Thirteen Never Changes

Other Apple Paperbacks
you will enjoy:

Afternoon of the Elves
by Janet Taylor Lisle

Turning Thirteen
by Susan Beth Pfeffer

The Broccoli Tapes
by Jan Slepian

Family Picture
by Dean Hughes

Thirteen Never Changes

Budge Wilson

AN
APPLE
PAPERBACK

SCHOLASTIC INC.
New York Toronto London Auckland Sydney

Originally published in Canada by Scholastic Canada Ltd.

ISBN 0-590-43488-8

12 11 10 9 8 7 6 5 4 3 2 1   1 2 3 4 5 6/9

Printed in the U.S.A.   28

First Scholastic printing, December 1991

To Sister Ruth Hennessey CSJ
Friend and Landlady

1

When Lorinda woke up that February morning, she sat up in bed and decided to think about funerals. She felt she needed to do a little thinking about funerals because she was going to be going to one in two days.

A few moments later, she realized that she didn't have a whole lot to think about. Because she'd never been to a funeral, she knew nothing about them. Well — almost nothing. Lorinda stared at the ceiling and revved up her thinking. What *did* she know?

Well, first of all, she thought (pretending she was making a list on a piece of paper), there is always someone dead at a funeral. Then, somewhere — in a church or in a house or in a mysterious place called a funeral home — a bunch of people come and do something. But what, exactly? Maybe it was sort of like church, with hymns and prayers and things, and probably the minister —

or priest or rabbi — said some holy things about the person, even if the person was a mean old witch. Or wizard, if he was a man.

Lorinda sighed. Her grandmother had been no witch, and would deserve the nice things that the minister would say. If he said she was a good woman who ought to go straight to heaven without even passing GO, Lorinda could believe it.

Lorinda got out of bed and padded over to the window to check the view. Every morning she did this. It was as though she wanted to make sure it was still there. She always tried to do it before Jessie was awake. Jessie was only five years old, and could gabble right through a sunrise, no matter how beautiful it was.

That morning the water in Blue Harbour was glassy calm, and there was almost no movement in the boats tied up to their club poles. Lorinda could see the lobster boats out on Albacore Bay stopping for a while and then chugging on to the next trap. For a moment she forgot about funerals, and enjoyed the bright stillness outside.

After she'd crawled back into bed for an extra ten minutes under the warm covers, Lorinda sighed again. Everything she knew about her grandmother was good, but she knew almost nothing. Grandma and Grandpa had only visited Lorinda's family twice. It took a long time and a lot of money to fly from Vancouver, where her grandparents lived, to Nova Scotia.

But when they had come, it had been special. Grandma had made the most amazing meringue tarts. Lorinda's mother never seemed to get them right, even with the recipe right in front of her. Grandma sang a lot, too (songs that Lorinda had never even heard before; they certainly weren't from 1989!), and she always brought presents. Last Christmas she'd sent Lorinda a little miniature totem pole.

Lorinda reached up to the shelf above her bed, and fished around till she found it. She brought it down and held it under the covers, rubbing her thumb over the strange faces and stiff wooden birds.

Then a big tear slid out from under one of her eyelids and ran down the side of her face into her ear.

"I'm not crying because I'll miss her," she whispered to the ceiling. "I'm crying because I didn't know her well enough to miss, and now it's too late. Now I'll never know her." She turned over in bed and sobbed into her pillow.

The door opened quietly, and her mother came in. She went over to the bed and sat down, smoothing Lorinda's long black hair away from her face and stroking it gently.

"Don't be too sad, Lorinda," she said — softly, so as not to waken Jessie, who was sleeping in her little bed on the other side of the room. "But have a good cry. It'll do you good. Thirteen years old isn't too old to cry. If you have a good reason, it's perfectly okay to cry, even if you're as old as Methuselah."

But Lorinda was cried out for the moment. She blew her nose hard and wiped her face with the end of the sheet. "You don't look so hot yourself, Mom," she said. "But then she's — she *was* — your mother. That must be *awful*. I hope you don't die till I'm a million years old."

Mrs. Dauphinee chuckled. "That'd make me pretty ancient!" She looked at Lorinda sadly. "Yes," she said. "It's hard to lose a mother. But the reason we shouldn't be *too* sad is that she'd been sick for a long, long time, and had a lot of pain. I think we should be willing to let her go."

"But, Mom." Lorinda thought she might start crying again. "I feel like I didn't even know her. And now I never will. I feel real bad now, because I didn't write her any letters except thank-you letters, and even when she was here, I didn't ask her any questions. Like what she was like when she was a kid. Or what was her favourite treat. Or what it was like to be your mother. Or how it feels to be sick all the time."

Mrs. Dauphinee took in a long breath and let it out slowly. "Well," she said, "I guess most of us have feelings like that when people die. We keep

4

saying, 'If only . . . if only I'd done this or that, or if only I'd had a chance to say goodbye.' " Mrs. Dauphinee's eyes filled with tears.

Lorinda took her hand out from under the covers and laid it on her mother's arm. She didn't know what to say, so she just kept her hand there for a while.

Then Mrs. Dauphinee said, "And she was so young."

"What?" Lorinda sat right up in bed. "How old was she?"

"Sixty-two," said her mother.

It was Lorinda's turn to chuckle. "Young! Sixty-two sounds like about a hundred to me. Like an old, old lady."

"Well, she wasn't. She had me when she was twenty-four, and you were born when I was twenty-five. If you have a baby when you're twenty-four, I'll be sixty-two when that child is your age. More or less."

Lorinda was grinning. "Wow, Mom, I sure understand why I'm good at math. It runs in the family!" Then she sobered up. "But, Mom! I don't like to think of you being sixty-two so soon!"

"Well, it's hardly soon," laughed her mother. "It's not like you'll be having that thirteen-year-old child tomorrow! Now c'mon. Get up. It's a beautiful day — the kind of day that makes you really glad to live in a Nova Scotia fishing village.

Besides, the plane leaves at eight-fifteen tomorrow morning, and we have a lot to do before we go. If the Himmelmans are going to look after Jessie while we're gone, I'd like to prepare a casserole for them, and maybe some brownies. It's no joke looking after someone who's five years old. I think the Himmelmans are going to need a little prize! And before we leave, we have to decide what to pack and what to leave behind."

James was at the doorway, rubbing his eyes. In the morning, he always looked as though he'd just crawled out of a hole. And he couldn't see halfway across the room until he put his glasses on.

"Think it'll be a good day for flying tomorrow?" he asked, his voice all muzzy.

Lorinda's heart did a little skip-hop, in spite of herself. Flying! She remembered back to two years before, when she and James had flown to Ontario to spend six terrible-wonderful months in Peterborough. It had been her first flight. She could hardly wait to get on a plane again.

"Mom," she asked, hesitating a little, "is it a really sinful thing for me to be looking forward to that airplane ride, when I should be thinking about Grandma's funeral?"

Mrs. Dauphinee patted her arm. "Of course it's not," she said. "Grandma would want you to enjoy it. The mountains and all. I'm looking forward to it myself." Then she paused before continuing. "Sometimes lovely things make you twice as sad when you're sorrowful — like music or sunsets or the sun sparkling on the bay this morning — but in a strange way those things can seem extra wonderful, too."

"Let's see." Lorinda leapt out of bed and went over to the window again. The view had changed since she'd first looked out. The sun was shining full on the long reaches of water that led to the open sea. The wind was starting to ruffle the surface just enough to catch the light, making it bounce and dance off the waves. In the distance, Lorinda could see Mr. Coolen steering his boat right through the path of light, heading home for breakfast after checking his nets.

It was one of those February mornings that can almost fool you into thinking that the winter's over. Lorinda could see some of the men standing around on the Government Wharf in their shirt sleeves, and Mrs. MacDermid was hanging out her wash with just her sweater on over her other clothes. Mom's right, thought Lorinda. It's extra beautiful, but there's an ache right in the centre of my chest, too.

"Very mysterious," said James.

"What is?"

"How you can feel sad and happy all at the same time."

"Right," agreed Lorinda. "Very mysterious."

By bedtime that night, the Dauphinees had finished most of their preparations for the trip. Glynis and George Himmelman had come over to collect Jessie and all her gear — her three dolls, her favourite bear, her small suitcase, her china cat. Even loaded down with a lot of other stuff, George had an arm free to hold the basket with Mrs. Dauphinee's casserole and brownies. He just sat the teddy bear down on top of it all.

"Don't you worry," said George. "Mom says to tell you we won't let Jessie out of our sight. And you know Glynis — she'd rather have Jessie than four dozen dolls."

Glynis was eight and Jessie was five, and both of them were so pleased to be together that they only turned around once to wave goodbye.

By six-fifteen the next morning, they were all packed and ready to go. Gretzky, Lorinda's big grey cat, would be fed by the MacDermids while they were away. Always sleepy, he hardly opened his eyes when Lorinda came to say goodbye. She picked him up and hugged him hard, kissing the top of his head.

"Don't do anything stupid while we're gone," she whispered. "Like get run over by a truck or anything." But Gretzky just purred a little louder and closed his eyes even tighter.

Then the MacDermid car was there in the driveway, with Mrs. MacDermid at the wheel. "Pile in," she yelled, as she got out to open up the trunk. "I almost had to tie Fiona and Duncan down to keep them from coming too, but there wasn't enough room. They can help their father in the shop."

The MacDermids ran a gift shop in the village. Duncan loved to wait on customers and, as Fiona put it, "make change and suggestions." Fiona was a red-hot gift-wrapper, and it was never boring for her to work in the store.

"Hurry, now!" cried Mrs. MacDermid, pushing James along. James never hurried. "We can't let you miss that plane." She was scratching behind her ear and pulling at her coat collar and tapping her foot up and down on the driveway. Lorinda watched her closely. Red hair, she was thinking, and twitchy nerves. How come Mr. MacDermid, who has red hair too, is as calm as the water on Tadpole Pond? I know it's really nice of Mrs. MacDermid to take us all to the airport, but I sure wish she could do it without making it seem like such a crisis.

Crisis was a word Lorinda had learnt two summers ago, when there'd been a whole lot of mysterious lights out on the Bay. Yes siree, Mrs. MacDermid sure knew how to make a crisis out of almost anything.

Lorinda thought back to the Christmas three

years ago, when she and James had set up a lemonade stand in the MacDermid store. They'd been trying to raise money for their mother's gift. Now, *there* was a day full of hot tempers! And not just Mrs. MacDermid's, either, Lorinda admitted to herself with a sad smile.

At last all the suitcases and coats and carry-on bags were stowed away, and Mrs. MacDermid was behind the wheel. "I don't know what on earth makes all of you Dauphinees so slow. Except maybe Lorinda. She's more like me." Lorinda didn't have time to think about that before Mrs. MacDermid turned the key in the ignition and put her foot on the gas. The car shot forward with a lurch. "At last!" she exclaimed, scratching that spot behind her ear again. "We're off!"

2

By seven-fifteen, they were at the airport. Mrs. MacDermid — full of suggestions and warnings — had left the Dauphinees, who were now sending their bags and purses through the X-ray machine.

"I hope they don't think that curling iron of yours is a gun, Mom," whispered Lorinda. "It sure looks exactly like one on the X-ray screen."

Mr. Dauphinee chuckled. "I imagine by now they can tell a gun from a curling iron," he said.

"Lookit," added James, pointing to the screen. "Ever see a gun with an electric cord on the end?" And Lorinda had to grin, in spite of feeling pretty stupid.

Mrs. Dauphinee handed them each a package when they got to the waiting room. "Here," she said. "From Mrs. MacDermid. Going-away presents."

"Oh dear!" moaned Lorinda.

"Oh dear what?" asked her mother.

"Now I feel guilty. For all the things I've been thinking."

"Like what?" James was curious.

"A lot of things. A bunch of stuff about Mrs. MacDermid. She really kind of drives me crazy, with all her jitters. She's always scratching and twitching, and it puts a knot in my stomach just being around her. Like she's always in such a big rush." She paused a minute, and then said, reluctantly, "Duncan's like that, too. Forever hurrying me, and making everything seem like such a big *production*. And Mrs. MacDermid gets so *mad* about things." She took a long breath. "I was just thinking how nice it was that she'd finally left, and here she's gone and given us presents." Lorinda put a hand over her face.

"And took us all to the plane, too," reminded her mother. "Seventy-five kilometres."

"I know. I *know*." That didn't make Lorinda feel any better.

James just sat there smiling.

"What are you grinning about?" snapped Lorinda.

But James just smiled some more.

"Oh James!" cried Lorinda. "You make me almost as furious as Mrs. MacDermid does. She's such a nervous wreck, and you're so doggone *calm*."

James chuckled. "Maybe I'm just too young to have much to twitch about yet. Ten isn't very ancient, y'know." Then he went right on smiling.

Lorinda looked hard at him. "Ten years is plenty old enough to be a pain in the neck," she said. "I know exactly what you're thinking. When you're thirteen years old, you get to be a mind reader."

"Okay, then," said James. "What am I thinking?"

"You're thinking that Lorinda Dauphinee has a pretty wild temper herself, and that the reason Mrs. MacDermid and I can't get along is that we're too much alike."

Just then a voice announced boarding time over the loudspeaker, and James didn't have to answer. They all dug out their boarding passes and set off for the plane.

The plane ride was long but wonderful — seven hours and fifty minutes, with a change of planes in Montreal. James and Lorinda took turns sitting by the window, and when they got to the Rocky Mountains, they were almost sitting on one another's laps. Flight attendants were forever bringing drinks or snacks or meals, as well as little pillows and magazines and small blankets if people felt cold. There were earphones for plugging yourself into different kinds of music, and in the afternoon the Dauphinees pulled down the blinds and watched a whole movie. Then, when time started to hang a little bit heavy on their hands, they took out Mrs. MacDermid's presents — a really tricky puzzle for James and a little pocket-sized game of checkers for Lorinda.

It's hard to believe, thought Lorinda, that you can just sit-sit-sit all day, and still be busy every minute. Time was flying by — like the plane — very, very quickly.

Mrs. Dauphinee was thinking that sit-sit-sitting was just about the nicest gift that anyone could have given her. She'd stayed awake for two nights worrying about her parents, then grieving for her mother; and then she'd worked hard for two days preparing for the trip. So far, she'd spent most of it wrapped up in one of the plane's red blankets, fast asleep.

James, true to form, passed a lot of the time thinking. "What are you when you're dead?" he asked Lorinda.

Lorinda stared at him for a moment. "How would I know? Anyway, what do you really mean?"

James frowned. "I'm not sure," he said. "I mean, before we were born we sort of *weren't*, but we weren't dead. We just weren't *here*. Now Grandma's not here, either. Is she the same as not born yet, or something else?"

"Lots of people," said Lorinda, "say you go to heaven when you die. Or somewhere else if you're very, very wicked."

"But what's *that*?"

"What's *what*?"

"What's heaven?" said James quietly, almost as though he were talking to himself. "I've been up above the clouds three times, and that's enough to tell me that heaven isn't there. Even if it was, I still wouldn't know what dead was."

"Well, I don't know, either," said Lorinda. "And you're not gonna find out by looking it up in some old encyclopedia. Maybe we'll just all of a sudden *know*, when . . ." She stopped speaking abruptly.

"When what?"

"When we see her. Grandma, I mean. Maybe we'll know what dead is then. James?" Lorinda was twisting one of the buttons on her sweater.

"Yeah?"

"James. I'm sort of . . . well, you know . . ."

"Yeah. Me too."

"Scared. A little bit scared."

"Yes."

"James, we never saw a dead person before. But I guess we have to now."

He sighed. "I guess so," he said.

In front of them, Mr. and Mrs. Dauphinee were both asleep. Their mother was snoring, ever so softly, almost like Gretzky purring.

"She'll probably just look asleep," said Lorinda. "Maybe."

"Yeah. Maybe."

"Darn it all anyway," announced Lorinda.

"Hmm?"

"Well, I just wish people didn't have to die. I don't see why God didn't arrange it so we could live on and on, forever."

James couldn't think of anything to say to that.

"But if people do have to die," continued Lorinda, "I wish they'd warn you, so you could write them letters and ask them a whole bunch of questions. It drives me crazy that my only grandmother has died and I didn't even really know her. That's *awful*."

"Yeah."

Just past noon, Pacific Time, they landed at Vancouver International Airport. Grandpa was there to greet them. He looked very old and tired and sad, and when Lorinda saw him, she felt like crying again.

Mrs. Dauphinee gave her father a big hug. "Thanks, Dad, for sending us the money for the trip," she said.

"That's okay," he mumbled. "I needed you here. All of you. When you get to the end of something, it does you good to remember that some things are only just beginning." He was looking at James and Lorinda.

My gosh, thought Lorinda, he really thinks that James and I are just beginning to live. I feel like I've been around forever!

But she didn't have time to think any more about it. They were driving into West Vancouver, and they could see mountains out the window — capped with snow, higher than they'd looked from the plane — and before long they saw the Lion's Gate Bridge, and the edge of Stanley Park.

Then Grandpa was speaking. "We'll eat some lunch before we go to the funeral home. There's enough food at home to feed the whole navy." Mrs. Dauphinee's father — Mr. Davison — had been in the navy before he retired, and he still thought about it a lot.

"Couldn't we go to the funeral home first?" suggested Lorinda. I'll never be able to eat a single thing, she thought, if I have to worry about that funeral home all through lunch.

"Right now?" Mr. Davison was surprised, but he patted her knee and said, "Okay, m'dear, if that's the way you want it."

When they reached the funeral home, Lorinda was surprised to see that it looked like a huge old house.

Inside, it was very quiet. Men in black suits stood around looking serious, and whispering. There were thick carpets everywhere, so thick you couldn't even hear your own footsteps. Outside one room there was a white book on a sort of stand. People were supposed to write their names in it, so that later on, Mr. Davison would know who had come to visit. In it, Mr. Dauphinee wrote:

Lydia and Jim Dauphinee
Lorinda and James

Lorinda grabbed James's hand as they entered. There were zillions of flowers in the room, and armchairs lined up along the walls. The light wasn't very bright, and there were candles on what used to be the mantelpiece.

Directly across from the doorway, Lorinda and James could see the coffin. Lorinda turned away quickly, and thought, do I *have* to? Do I have to look? James was staring at the carpet, and probably, guessed Lorinda, thinking the very same thing.

Mr. and Mrs. Dauphinee walked slowly over to the coffin, but James and Lorinda stayed by the door. "Come along, kids," said Grandpa, with a crack in his voice. "Come and have a last look at your Grandma. The coffin will be closed for the funeral tomorrow." Then he took each of them by the hand and led them over. "She looks very peaceful," he added. "Just like she's having a nice deep sleep."

Lorinda forced her eyes to look, and there was her grandmother's body, dressed in a navy blue silk dress with a white collar. The fluffy hair looked like it always had when she was alive. But nothing else did.

Lorinda stared and stared. She doesn't look like she's sleeping at all, she thought. In fact, she doesn't look either peaceful or unpeaceful. She just looks *gone*.

"She's left," said Lorinda, right out loud.

"Yes," agreed James. "Not here. Not any more."

Then some other people came into the room. Grandpa introduced the Dauphinees and they talked for a while. Lorinda and James went over and sat on two of the armchairs to wait, wishing that this part of their visit would hurry up and be over.

And soon it was. The other people left, and Mr. and Mrs. Dauphinee went over to take one last look at the coffin. Mrs. Dauphinee was crying a little. Grandpa came over to put his arm around her, and he was crying, too. It was as though the two of them were all alone in the world. Mr. Dauphinee went and sat beside James and Lorinda.

"It's like Mom doesn't even know we're here, or that we need her," said Lorinda.

"She's got a whole bunch of things she's needing herself right now," said James.

"That's right, James," agreed his father. "We're

so used to having her look after the four of us that sometimes it's hard to realize that she might need a little looking after herself."

"But how can we do that?" asked Lorinda.

"Well," said her dad, rubbing his jaw and thinking, "we could maybe start by giving her a little breathing space. Tomorrow'll be a tough day for her, it being the funeral and all. And she's tired anyway. So the best thing we can do is try not to pounce on her the minute we need help for ourselves. After all, there are three of us. That's a good-sized support system. We can help each other during that time. Eh, troops?"

James and Lorinda grinned at their father, and said, "Yes, *sir!*" Then they all left the room and went out to the hall to get their coats and boots. At the door, Mr. Davison and Mrs. Dauphinee both turned around and took one last slow look at the room — at the flowers, the empty armchairs, the silent coffin.

3

Afterwards, the day of the funeral seemed like a dream to Lorinda. It was peculiar enough to be living in an unfamiliar place in a strange city. It was stranger still to be watching their mother looking after her own father instead of her and James.

The drive to the church was silent and awful, but the music in the church was so beautiful that Lorinda had to chew her lips and count the candles to keep from crying.

The closed coffin was brought up to the front, and the minister gave them a little sermon about how good a woman Grandma had been, and how she'd go straight to heaven and live in one of those "many mansions" that the Bible talked about. Why isn't she there already, wondered Lorinda, since she certainly left here before we even arrived? Oh well, maybe she's on her way. Those big houses may be a long way off.

She sighed. She couldn't quite imagine her grandmother checking into one. She liked things sort of simple. Like the Dauphinee house in Blue Harbour, for instance.

Somewhere out there beyond her thoughts, Lorinda knew they were saying the 23rd Psalm. *Yea though I walk through the valley of the shadow of death, I will fear no evil. For Thou art with me.* But she tried not to listen, for fear she'd cry. She hated crying if people could see her doing it. Next to her, James was sniffling, his hands in his lap, tears streaming down his cheeks. Lorinda handed him her handkerchief. "Blow!" she whispered fiercely in his ear. "But keep one corner clean, in case I need it myself."

Then came "Abide With Me," a hymn that often made Lorinda feel like crying, even when she had nothing to cry about. *Fast falls the eventide.* Lorinda started counting again — this time, the tiny panes of glass in the huge stained glass window behind the choir.

At last they were out of the church and into the silent car again. Then came the cemetery part, with the minister quoting comforting pieces out of the Bible, while the coffin was lowered onto the stand above the grave.

The day was cold and wet, and rain dripped off the trees. James was hanging on tight to Mr. Dauphinee's hand, and Mrs. Dauphinee had her arm around her father. Lorinda was hugging herself with both arms, her face like a stone. If I don't think, she said to herself, I'll maybe be okay. Like not think about how cold it must be down in that hole in the middle of February. But then she figured that it didn't really matter, because Grandma had left, some time ago. But where was she now? Where? Where? One of the many mansions appeared in Lorinda's imagination, but she shoved it away.

Then another silent drive, and at last they were back at the house to have a . . . sort of a . . . party. Yes, a party. People were solemn and quiet at first, but then there was even some laughter here and there, and Lorinda saw that her mother was eating a butter tart and smiling at someone.

Lorinda felt the knot in her stomach loosen a little. Tomorrow they'd be on the plane again, and all of this would be only a memory. "Yes," she said to a man who had just come up to speak to her. "Yes, we do live on the East Coast . . . Yes it is. Very nice . . . No, we don't have mountains. Not honest-to-goodness ones . . ." (Had this man never taken any geography?) ". . . Yes, I do like flying . . . No, it isn't scary, not any more. It used to be, when I was young." At that, the man laughed, and moved on.

A woman came over and sat down beside Lorinda.

"My dear," crooned the woman, "how sad for you that your poor granny is dead."

"Yes," said Lorinda. "But we called her Grandma."

"Well, grandma, then." The woman was looking less friendly, but was still trying. "It must be very hard for you to be missing such a dear, dear friend."

"Well, ma'am," said Lorinda, "my biggest problem is that she wasn't my dear, dear friend. Not really. I didn't hardly know her at all."

Lorinda was just about to ask the woman some questions about her grandmother, but the lady seemed uncomfortable with this conversation. "I think I'll go find a sandwich," she said hurriedly, and returned to the table in the dining room.

After a while, everyone left, except the Dauphinees and Mr. Davison. A group of men and women had cleaned up the dishes and put the food away, and now the family was alone in the living room of Grandpa's house, and it was quiet again.

Grandpa sank into a chair and heaved a long sigh. Mrs. Dauphinee sat beside him and held his hand. But then suddenly he sat up straight and smiled at all of them.

"A few weeks before she died," he said to Mrs. Dauphinee, "your mother gave me some instructions about things she wanted me to give people — things that were special treasures of hers.

For instance, Julia Shultz, her best friend, is to have the cameo brooch that her mother gave her. You, Lydia, are to have her best rings — her wedding and engagement rings, and a locket that belonged to her grandmother. Jim — you get the silver cufflink box that she always kept her earrings in. Maybe you can use it for stamps or something.

"James — " he smiled at his grandson and his voice was unsteady, "you and she were big gardeners. She knew how much you liked to grow flowers, even in the winter. So she left you her collection of gardening books — what she called her 'How-To' books — you know, How To Grow Poppies, How To Make a Rock Garden, How To Water a Flower Without Drowning It — stuff like that. She used to read those books in bed, when most people would be reading whodunnits or watching TV." Grandpa was silent for a few moments before continuing.

"Jessie is to have the amethyst ring that she wore on her little finger. The stone came from Blomidon in Nova Scotia, near where she used to live when she was a girl — long before I took her off to live in places all over the country when I was in the navy.

"But Lorinda," — and he looked at her where she sat in the chair opposite him, eyes bright, trying not to look too interested or hopeful —

"she had a kind of special interest in you. It wasn't that she loved you better than the other grand-children, but she had a feeling that you and she were a lot alike."

Lorinda thought about that. How could such a thing be? Grandma had always seemed so gentle and sort of patient. But she'd better listen to what Grandpa was saying.

"She looked a lot like you when she was a kid, and, well, I think she was kind of lively and, ah . . ."

Lorinda helped him. "A little bit short-fused, as Mom says about me? I bet not."

"I bet so," he chuckled. "Grandparents always like to seem especially calm and serene and perfect when they're with their grandchildren. And they see them so seldom that it isn't really all that hard to fool them into thinking those things. But un-derneath everything, we're just ordinary people, you know."

Lorinda was staring at him. Now she *knew* she hadn't known her grandmother, not even a little.

"Your grandmother," he continued, "learned to control her temper better and better as she grew older. But, boy!" — and here he grinned — "she was a pretty fiery customer when I first married her. Sometimes I wondered what I'd got myself into. But it was okay. She was fun and warm and loving, and I happen to know that you're like that too. So . . ."

Lorinda found herself saying, "So?"

"So she left you what was maybe her most precious set of possessions. She asked me to give you all her diaries."

"Her *diaries!*" whispered Lorinda. "Full of *secrets.*"

Mr. Davison laughed. "Right. Full of secrets. In fact, she said to me, with that glint in her eye, sick though she was, 'Lorinda's to get those diaries, and I'll tell you something else. You're not to open a single one of them, even to page two. I don't want you spending your old age worrying about all those old boyfriends, all those old secrets.' "

"But won't she . . . wouldn't she . . . mind me reading all that stuff?"

"Apparently not. She said, 'Lorinda's young, and Lorinda's a woman, and what's more, she'll understand what I've written about. Because she's a lot like me.' "

Lorinda sat there and repeated over and over to herself the words *Lorinda's a woman.* What a strange proud feeling. Then she said, "How many are there?"

"A lot," said her grandfather. "And some are pretty big. She soon stopped trying to squeeze herself onto the pages of those tiny little diaries with locks and keys. She just went to the stationery stores and bought big black hardcover notebooks.

"There's a whole box full of them upstairs. I don't know how you'll get them all back to Nova Scotia."

"Don't you worry, Grandpa," Lorinda said hurriedly. "We'll get them there just fine — even if I have to throw all the clothes out of my suitcase." She shook her head and frowned. "No way I'm gonna trust those precious things to the mail system."

"There!" exclaimed Grandpa. "Laura was right. She said you'd value them and you do. Before you see even the outside covers of them."

Lorinda watched him, eyes shining. Then, suddenly she jumped out of the chair and clapped her hands.

"Hey!" she breathed. "D'you know what this means? Oh my gosh — it means I get a second chance! I've been so sad because I didn't know Grandma better before she died. But by the time I finish those diaries, I'll know her extremely well — maybe better than any of you do . . . did."

Grandpa was watching her, smiling a sad thin smile.

"And Grandpa!"

"Yes?"

"I keep a diary too. I know what it's all about."

"I know," said Grandpa. "*She* knew."

Lorinda sighed and went over to sit on the floor beside her grandfather. She put her hand on his knee and laid her head against his leg. She wanted to say something, but she wasn't sure she could say it and look him in the eye, all at the same time. So she just stared at the carpet.

"Grandpa?"

"Yes?"

"Thank you. And something else."

"Yes?"

"I'm real sorry and sad for you. Because, well . . ."

"Because?"

"Because you've just lost Grandma, and that makes me feel awful. But I feel extra sad for you because . . . I've just found her."

She jumped up and ran out of the living-room and upstairs to the guest room. Then she threw herself down on the bed and had a good noisy cry. It was a strange cry — full of gratitude and regret, relief and pain. But at least it was more satisfactory than the crying she had been doing. When it was over, Lorinda turned on her back and stared at the ceiling.

Calm and steady, she said, "Thank you, Grandma."

4

"**W**hy does Grandpa look so much older than Grandma did?" asked Lorinda on the plane the next day.

"Because he *is* older," said her mother, who was sitting beside her. "Not much, but some. And he's having a very sad time. That makes everyone look older."

"He looks as old as the hills to me," sighed Lorinda. "How will he ever manage to look after himself? Laundry and meals and stuff?"

Mrs. Dauphinee paused before she answered. "I don't know. Mind you, he's used to doing a lot of those things, because Mother was sick for so long. But he probably doesn't realize yet how lonely he'll be. She was sick, but she was at home. *There* all the time. Oh, dear!" Mrs. Dauphinee put her hands over her face for a moment. "Wait'll he realizes how empty a house can seem when there's just one person in it. He doesn't even have a dog or a cat."

"Maybe we could . . ." started Lorinda, but then her voice trailed off. After all, how could Grandpa come and live at their house, when there was hardly enough room for just the five of them? "No," she continued. "I guess we couldn't."

Mrs. Dauphinee patted her knee. "Don't worry about it," she said. "Your dad and I are trying to work something out."

"Seems to me like he'd be easy to live with."

Again her mother paused. "Not always," she said, very quietly. "Mother was the one with the temper, even if you find it hard to believe. But Dad often got — still gets — what the family always called 'the glooms.' He gets sad and depressed easily — too easily. And he's a bit of a hypochondriac."

"A what?"

"A person who thinks he's sick when he's perfectly fine. If he gets a headache, he thinks he's dying, and wants the whole world to know. And if he gets a hangnail, he's sure he's got a terminal disease."

"Terminal?"

"Terminal means a disease you die from."

"Oh."

"I'm telling you all this so you'll know that it's

not a simple decision, asking him to live with us. And he can hardly go to Aunt Joan's in Halifax. She's got five kids and is expecting a sixth — and it could be twins. That's why she couldn't go to Vancouver with us. And my brothers are bachelors. Worse still, they live too far away. Dad wouldn't want to live in Venezuela or Scotland."

Lorinda looked anxiously at her mother. "Do you think they'll be all right?"

"What? Who? What are you talking about? The twins? My brothers?"

"No. The diaries. Do you suppose they're safe?"

Mrs. Dauphinee laughed. "You *are* like Grandma!" she said. "Always switching subjects in the middle of a conversation. She could be talking about horses, and all of a sudden she'd say, 'I think we should buy one.' I'd say, 'What? A horse?' and she'd say, 'No, silly. A TV set.' If you laughed at her, she'd always say there was a connection. And if you asked her what it was, she could usually tell you."

"Okay, then," said Lorinda. "How do you get from horses to TV sets?"

"Oh, that one would be easy. She'd say something like this: 'I was thinking how much I loved horses — all kinds — thoroughbreds, work horses, old tired horses. Then I thought about race horses, and how I've never seen a horse race. While I was feeling sorry about that, I thought,

I bet they show horse races on TV. So I said I think we should buy one.' Television sets were new enough then that not everyone had one."

"Wow!" cried Lorinda. "Do you suppose my mind works like that, too?"

"Well — how did you get from Aunt Joan's five children — or my brothers — to the safety of your diaries?"

"Holy!" Lorinda threw up her hands helplessly. "I dunno." But then she sat still and thought for a while. "I was — let's see — thinking that Aunt Joan had a lot of kids. And then I wondered what it'd be like to have a baby. I mean to have a baby be born. Then I wondered if it was harder to have a baby in Grandma's time than now. Like, did they have special doctors and special hospitals for having babies? And then I thought, I know how I can find out — the diaries! Then I started to worry about them being safe down there with all the other suitcases, even though the big black one Grandpa put them in is big and leather and strong — and locked."

Mrs. Dauphinee chuckled. "They'll be fine. Believe me, the bottom isn't going to fall out of this plane. And if it does, suitcases aren't the only things that will land in the middle of Lake Superior. We'll all be dead ducks, and dead ducks don't read diaries."

Lorinda laughed. "Would Aunt Marion ever

have been shocked by what you just said — before she changed. She was horrified that you let us travel by plane at all — she was that scared of them. But imagine how she'd feel about a mother who joked about being drowned!"

It was seven-thirty when they arrived at Halifax International Airport, and when they came down the escalator into the terminal, there was Mrs. MacDermid, pacing up and down in front of the luggage carousel.

All the way to Blue Harbour, Lorinda was very quiet. Not only was she not talking, she also wasn't listening very much. Even when Mrs. MacDermid listed all the news of the past three days, Lorinda heard with only half an ear. "Yes," Mrs. MacDermid was saying. "A big blow came up without any warning at all, and quite a few people lost a lot of traps. So sad, after all that work making them. I just bet a bunch of yours are gone, Jim. Just think of all those lobsters sitting on the bottom of the sea where no one can get at them. Someone should invent ropes that don't break. My word, there were enough lobster buoys washed up on Elbow Beach to keep the whole village supplied for a winter."

Then Mrs. MacDermid told about how Jessie spilled cake batter all over Mrs. Himmelman's floor, but how she and Jessie cleaned it all up.(Babble, babble, babble, thought Lorinda.) And how Gretzky was such a nice cat that she was thinking of getting a kitten. And how Duncan was getting more and more bossy, and how even George Himmelman was getting fed up with him.

"If he doesn't watch out," Mrs. MacDermid said, "even Lorinda will start getting mad at him."

Lorinda looked at the back of Mrs. MacDermid's head and grinned. *Start* getting mad at him, she thought. I've been a little bit mad at him for about six months. He's always been my best friend in Blue Harbour, but darn it, I sure get tired of being bossed around like I was a private and he was the general. No wonder Fiona gets so frantic. He treats *her* like she isn't even *there*. He was always kind of, well, pushy. But it seems like the minute he got to be thirteen, he thought he had to act like he was thirty-five and the Chairman of the Board. And when I got to be thirteen last week, he couldn't see that it was a big thing at all. When we do something together — just me and him or the whole gang — it's always gotta be *his* game or *his* suggestion.

Lorinda sighed. She wished everything could be smooth sailing for once. Just when Reginald Corkum looked like he might stop being such a horror story, Duncan had to go and start being a pain. Why can't he be more like that calm, patient father of his, she thought, and less like his mother?

"Lorinda!" This was Mrs. MacDermid speaking, and Lorinda had a horrible feeling she'd spoken to her before. "Lorinda!"

"Yes? What, Mrs. MacDermid?"

"My land! Gathering wool again! Do I have to shriek to get your attention?"

"I'm sorry, Mrs. MacDermid."

"Well, okay Lorinda, I was wondering why you didn't cut your hair. I think it would improve your looks a lot — sort of lift your face, you know."

Lorinda felt rage rising inside her. Improve my looks, eh? Meaning, I suppose, that they are in grave need of improvement. Well, I like my long hair — even if you think my face would look better lifted. Boy, I sure see how Duncan got that way.

"I *like* long hair," said Lorinda coldly, and Mrs. MacDermid frowned.

Mrs. Dauphinee was floundering around in the front seat, trying to smooth everything over. "I'm sure Mrs. MacDermid didn't mean . . . of course we all like your hair the way it is . . . maybe sometime when you're older you'll want to change it . . ." On and on and on. Lorinda felt another stab of annoyance. Why was her mother always

36

and forever trying to fix everything? And worrying, always *worrying*. About Dad's health. Her safety. Grandpa's nerves.

What's wrong with me? Lorinda sat up a little straighter, and thought about that. I'm a bad person, I guess. She sighed. Mad at everybody these days, and mixed up like a pan of hash. Things just don't seem to be simple any more. In the old days, there were good guys and bad guys. Good guys — Mom and Dad and the family and Duncan and the other kids and Sarah. Bad guys — Reginald Corkum and Mildred and Aunt Marion. Now it's like everyone's trying to confuse me. The good guys are starting to look not so perfect after all. And the bad guys are mixing me up almost as much by sometimes turning out to be nice. Like even Reginald is a little bit nice. And Aunt Marion got to be someone I loved a whole lot. Even Mildred. Look what happened to her that summer two years ago. Lorinda sighed again.

"What's the matter?" asked James, who'd been snoozing for most of the ride.

"Oh, I dunno," she said. "I'm just finding life kind of crazy right now." She thought a minute. "I know I've only been thirteen for two weeks, but it's a whole lot different from being twelve."

"How?"

"Well, twelve is still one hundred percent kid.

Thirteen is putting your big toe into something else. Into being a tiny bit grown up. You'll see. Wait'll it happens to you. But it isn't that simple."

"How come?"

"It's not like you're *really* old. So you're not young and you're not old, and it's like you don't fit anywhere. And you see too much. You notice too much. People start to make you mad for things you didn't even know were happening before. Even people you like a whole lot."

"Don't worry about it," said her mother, who seemed to have heard everything, right through Mrs. MacDermid's non-stop conversation. "The funeral was hard for all of us. And we're all suffering from jet lag. Look at your father. He's been asleep ever since we left the airport."

There she goes again, thought Lorinda. Trying to fix everything. *And what's wrong with that? She's just trying to help me.* But none of us would need fixing, if Mrs. MacDermid hadn't been yattering and yattering ever since we got in the car. *And if we weren't in the car she so kindly provided, we'd still be sitting in the airport.* What is James looking so blasted calm about? *You know darn well, Lorinda Dauphinee, that if James wasn't around being calm all the time, you'd probably fall right apart at the seams at least once a week.* There's Duncan waiting for us outside our barn. Probably getting ready to tell me what he's decided we should do tomorrow. *Lorinda! He's your best friend!*

When the car stopped in front of the Dauphinee house, everyone piled out and started unloading the trunk. Even Jessie and Glynis, who appeared from behind the hedge, screaming their hellos, helped. It took both Mr. Dauphinee and Duncan to carry the suitcase of diaries upstairs.

When all the gear was safely inside, Lorinda said, "Thanks, Mrs. MacDermid. Thanks, Duncan," and walked right in the house and straight upstairs.

"What's wrong with *her*?" frowned Duncan.

"Nothing, really," explained Mrs. Dauphinee. "She's just tired."

"An odd sort of child," said Mrs. MacDermid to Duncan as they got in the car.

Up in her room, Lorinda closed her door and unlocked the big black suitcase.

There they were. The diaries. She picked up one that had a large red 13 written on the front. The 13 was printed in a fancy way on a square of white paper, which was stuck in the middle of the black cover. All around the 13 were flowers in bright colours, and a little ladybug sat in the centre of one of them. Lorinda slowly opened the book and started to read.

Dear Diary: Now that I'm thirteen, those little diaries aren't big enough to hold everything I want to say. So I bought this big black book. Now I feel like I can stretch myself. And I think I'm going to need that. I've only been thirteen for four hours, but already I feel different.

Lorinda chuckled to herself. "I don't believe it!" she said, right out loud. Then she went on reading.

Someone told me they thought thirteen was <u>the real beginning of life</u>. Before that you're just a little child who does things without thinking. But at thirteen you start to <u>know</u>. Understand what I mean, dear Diary? Not all the knowing is totally marvelous. Some of it is really bad stuff. But it's very exciting. This has been a beautiful birthday. I got a new bicycle. Red, and a two-wheeler of course. I never had one before. Eileen gave me a locket with room for two pictures in it. Do you know what she said? "You can put a picture of your husband in it, and your first child. But in the meantime, I stuck a picture of me on one side and Groucho on the other." Groucho's her dog. Eileen is the greatest best friend in the world. We call ourselves *The Siamese Twins.*

I wish we had a dog, and I'm mad at Mother because she says dogs are too much work, and anyway they smell. And make puddles when they're puppies. So we can't have one. Mother is too clean and thinks too much about things like bad smells and germs.

I usen't to mind about things like that. About being too clean, I mean. I just liked hugging Mother and loving her. But now I do mind. I wonder why. I guess it has something to do with that knowing stuff that starts to happen when you're thirteen.

Happy Birthday, dear Diary. It's your birthday too. My first diary came on my tenth birthday, from Granny, and was little and also pale blue, with a key to lock it. I put silly kid things in it, but maybe it'll be fun to read in my old age.

But I've got a whole lot more to say, now. Now that I'm thirteen. Now that I'm in my teens. I can tell you a thousand secrets, and nobody but you and me will ever know what they are.

Yours in great anticipation,
Laura

*   *   *

Lorinda closed the book and sat on the edge
of her bed, holding the diary close to her chest.
"Nobody but you and me and Lorinda," she
said.

5

The next day was Saturday, and Lorinda knew what she wanted to do with that lovely long empty day. She wanted to go up to her room and open up that black book with the big 13 written on it. She wanted to crawl under her quilt — made by her father's mother, her other grandmother who had died when she was four — and read the book from cover to cover. So she went downstairs in her pyjamas and dressing gown instead of getting dressed. She'd hardly got halfway through her bran flakes when Duncan burst in the back door.

Don't knock or anything.

"Hi, Lorinda! What're you doing sitting around the kitchen in your pyjamas? On a Saturday, for pete's sake!"

None of your business. "I'm eating my breakfast. What does it look like?"

"Well, okay. You don't have to bite my head

off! But get a move on! You and me are going skating this morning on Black Lake. The ice is terrific. We gotta get out there fast and use it before it gets chewed up by a million pairs of skates. So that's what we're gonna do!"

"Oh, are we, now?" Lorinda heard the cold words coming out of her without even planning them.

"What? What're you talking about?" Lorinda couldn't decide whether Duncan looked mad or hurt.

"Lookit, Duncan," sighed Lorinda. "I guess I'm kinda tired. Jet lag and all. And the funeral. And it's just that sometimes I like to make up my own mind about what I'm going to do with my Saturdays. And today I think I'm gonna read all day."

"Read!"

"Yes. Read. I've got a really interesting . . . book . . . to finish, and I think it'll probably take all day. Sorry."

"But the weatherman wants snow for tomorrow."

"So?"

"So it'll cover up all that ice."

"Well then, go skate on it today. We can't very well both read my book." We sure can't.

"Oh, Lorinda!" Duncan stamped his foot on the door mat. "I don't see why you can't — "

"Sorry, Duncan." Lorinda got up and swished

her breakfast dishes in the warm soapy water that was waiting in the sink. Without turning around, she said, "I'm not gonna change my mind."

Duncan stomped out, banging the door shut behind him. *Like mother, like son.*

Lorinda climbed up the stairs and looked into her room. A nice cosy place to be, she thought. She went in and carefully closed the door behind her. Jessie was over playing with Ivan, and James was coasting down Mr. Hyson's icy hill with Glynis and Fiona. She wouldn't be disturbed before noon, and it was only eight-thirty. She looked out the window and tried to ignore the little frog pond in the field next door. The surface was like glass. There'd been a thaw when they'd been in Vancouver, but a sudden cold snap had refrozen the lakes to a black hardness. Lorinda could almost feel the surface under her feet; she loved to skate, and knew it would be perfect. If only Duncan had *asked* instead of *told*. "Hey, Lorinda, how'd you like to go skating this morning?" Like that. She sighed, and picked up the diary. Then she plumped up her pillows and crawled into the bed.

"Okay, Grandma," she said aloud. "Let's go!" She started to read.

Dear Diary: Sometimes I wish we'd never moved to Halifax, even though Eileen's here and she's my best friend now. But I really liked Wolfville. It was small enough that you could walk everywhere. Today I had to go to the dentist, and it took practically all day. Those yellow streetcars jiggling along on their tracks were fun before the war started. But now they always seem to be full to busting. You can't even sit and look out the window. And it isn't just servicemen. There are ordinary people by the ton.

I asked Mother why, and she said Halifax is fuller than full because there are thousands of men stationed here — women, too — and a lot of them have their families with them. She said the population has jumped from 60,000 to 100,000 since the war started. How can that be? Halifax is mostly just a peninsula. Seems to me it was pretty full before. It's a wonder people aren't dropping off the edges into the harbour.

Eileen says that it might have been easier to get to the dentist in Wolfville, but that Wolfville isn't exciting. Not like Halifax. You should see Bedford Basin, dear Diary. Sometimes it's got about 200 ships in it, all waiting to go to England with their terrible cargoes — guns and bombs and hand grenades. And with unterrible things like food and people.

When it's time to leave, the ships slowly sail out of the basin and through the harbour and down to the open sea. They go together in what's called a convoy, so if a submarine sinks one of them, they can help one another. And maybe chase the submarine. Or warship, or whoever did it. When a convoy leaves, it's a BIG SECRET, so the enemy won't know about it and rush out to sink them all.

But I think they're stupid if they think nobody knows. For goodness sake, people line up around the top of the Citadel to watch. Half the city knows. If I live to be a hundred, I'll never forget the look of those big parades of ships heading out to sea.

I guess Eileen is right. Things like that don't happen in Wolfville. Cows and apple trees and high tides just aren't in the same league as convoys.

Excuse me while I go get some bread and peanut butter.

Hi. I'm back.

Dad was in the last war — what they used to call the Great War. They also called it the War To End All Wars. Isn't that sad?

Because here we are in the middle of another one. Sometimes I ask Dad to tell me about that war, but he won't. He says it was too awful to talk about, and starts to look kind of sick. I don't see why. It couldn't all have been gruesome. There must have been exciting times, too, when men did big heroic things. I'd like to hear about that.

I wish I could be a spy in this war. I know I'm too young, but I think I'd do a really good job, and I'd never be scared. I'd creep up dark alleyways in Europe and steal enemy secrets and bring them back to our own army so they could win battles easier.

Once I told this to Dad, and he said, kind of sharply, "Girls can't be spies." Then, as I left the room, I heard him say to himself, "Or at least I hope not." I don't talk to him about it any more.

Listen, dear Diary. This is a new kind of diary. Not like the old ones, where I said things like "I went to school and got 90 in spelling and went to Eileen's birthday party and came home and had baked beans and cole slaw for supper." Those are EVENTS. In this diary I'm going to talk about my THOUGHTS, too. This will take *up a lot of time. Space, too. So I can't write every single day, or I'd have to give up the whole rest of my life. I'll just pick up my diary (you) and write something when I feel a thought coming over me. So I won't put in any dates, because one of my entries might take four weeks to write. I just tell you this so you won't be confused.*

The day war was declared, Dad just sat by the radio with his head in his hands. If he hadn't been a man, I would have thought he was crying.

This is a good place to stop. I've run out of thoughts.

Sincerely, Laura

From her bed, Lorinda looked out the window and tried to imagine the Bay full of warships. Bedford Basin was smaller than the Bay. It must have looked like a can of sardines with all those grey ships packed into it.

Lorinda wished she'd lived way back then when exciting things were happening. It wasn't that she wanted there to be a war now. Everyone, including her, worried a lot about nuclear bombs. They didn't have those back then, she thought. It must have been an easy kind of war. Just shooting and stuff. No big cities disappearing in a single giant puff in one terrible moment.

At least, not until the very end of the war, Lorinda said to herself, remembering Hiroshima and Nagasaki — the cities that had been destroyed by atom bombs. She felt sick. Like Grandma's dad. Better find out more about that war, she thought. So she got out of bed and checked in her encyclopedia. *Second World War — 1939–1945*, she read. Grandma must have been writing her diary around 1940 or maybe later. From now on, when I write in my diaries, I'm going to put dates on the pages. The year, anyway. Then my granddaughter will know the exact time I'm talking about.

She picked up the diary again and turned the page.

Dear Diary: I haven't written for almost a week, because we've been so busy. We've been making all sorts of changes in the house, like moving furniture around. And fixing up the spare room to make it really pretty.

You'll never guess what's going to happen! It's so wonderful that I can hardly believe it. We're going to get an English Guest Child. A girl. Did you ever hear anything more exciting? It's nice to have a big brother like Norman, who's seventeen, but brothers are boys, and besides he's too old to be of much real use to me. And Eric is such a pest he doesn't even count as a member of the family. I remember him being cute when he was about four, but I sure would like to know what happens to boys when they get to be nine. He's all the time yelling instead of talking, and he jumps out from behind doors and scares the stuffing out of me, and he makes fun of everything I do. He's forever rolling his eyes up to the ceiling and saying, "Girls! What drips!"

But even though Norman is old, and a boy, he's my hero. He talks to me like I was as grown up as he is, and he tells me stuff about high school. He says he's going to enlist in the navy when he's eighteen, but not to tell Dad. Or anybody. I can hardly wait. It'll be scary, but it'll be very beautiful thinking about his sacrifice, and his brave deeds. I'll watch from Citadel Hill when his convoy sails, and tears will quietly flow down my cheeks. When he returns from the war, the whole family will go down to the waterfront to watch him arrive — because there won't be secrets any more when the war is over — and maybe there'll be a band playing. And I'll point him out to everybody and say, "That's my brother. He's home from the war."

But until that happens, I have this other thing to look forward to. The Guest Child is the same age as me. Thirteen. Her name is Hilary Sutcliffe, and she lives in the south of England, not far from London, where there is a lot of bombing. English people are sending their children out of the cities into the country to keep them safe — even across the sea to places where there are no bombs at all. Like here in Canada. Hilary's father is in the airforce, and now her mother can go live nearer his base, and look after him when he's not up flying bombers.

She must be so proud of her father. But I'm glad my dad has an old war wound that keeps him here with us. His knee was smashed by a grenade or something, and he has a terrible limp. It's awful, but it's better than having him go miles and miles away. I feel like we need him here. He's sort of young. Not really, but young enough to enlist. He was only twenty-one when the last war ended. Mr. Sutcliffe is lots younger. He wasn't even in the *last war at all. He's only thirty-four.*

Have to go to bed. Imagine. I'm about to have a real live half-adopted sister.

Laura

Lorinda had forgotten all about the ice. Duncan or no Duncan, it would have taken six horses to drag her out of that bed. She was in it, and she was going to stay in it until she met Hilary.

Dear Diary: All week we've been painting Hilary's walls, and yesterday we went down and bought a cute little new rug for her floor. It's mauve with pink roses embedded in the fuzz, and it's soft to put your feet on when you get out of bed. I'm a little bit jealous, because my own rug is old as the ark, but Mother says we have to make things extra nice for her because she'll be so far from her parents and probably homesick. So she deserves the mauve rug. And when she goes back to England after the war, I bet I can have it then.

I'll be such a wonderful sister to Hilary! I'm going to try really hard to help her feel happy here. Before I go to sleep at night, I like to daydream about what I'll do for her. Like lend her clothes if she can't bring much over in her suitcase, and stand up for her if any of the kids at school are mean. In one of my best daydreams, I'm knocked unconscious by Henry Macdonald when I scold him for teasing Hilary on her way home. Mr. Brown (handsome), the vice-principal of Tower Road School — which is on our street — comes out and carries me tenderly into his office. Usually in the dream, Hilary weeps with gratitude.

Hilary's probably pretty, because I've read in stories that English girls always have beautiful skin. Mine is awful. Not pimply, but muddy-looking. English girls have pink cheeks. I look as though I need a blood transfusion. But Eileen says I have good bones. She's always loyal, and knows how to make me feel better when I'm in the dumps.

Today I got so mad at Eric that I thought I'd burst into about six pieces, with my arms and legs and body and head all landing in different parts of the room. He borrowed my bicycle without asking, and he's too short to ride it. He's mad because he hasn't got a two-wheel bike. He took it out and rode it all over the Dalhousie University grounds, and then fell off when he went over a bump. The bike went right on without him, and broke three spokes when it ran into a tree. A lot of the red paint got scraped off, too. When he told me, I jumped on the elevator tower he'd made with his Meccano set, and squashed it all up. He cried and cried, and I said, "See what happens to little squirts of brothers when they steal things!"

Later Norman came and sat on my bed, and said just two things. He didn't scold and rant or anything. He just said, very quietly, "Eric had to have six stitches in his knee." Then he said, "When you were nine years old, you took my bike one day and rode it for three hours — without asking."

I said, "Did I break it?"

He said, "No."

I said, "_Well_?"

He said, "Well what?"

I said, "Well, that's a _big difference_."

He said, "Not really. He didn't _mean_ to hurt your bike. He's just not very well coordinated. He was born that way. You and I are athletic. Not him."

I said, "Oh phooey!" But later on I thought about it. That's the trouble with being thirteen. You're all the time _thinking_ about things. Like nothing's simple any

*more. Before, it was like this: broken bike
equals bad brother. Now I have to divide
the whole sum by his bad co-ordination and
my own past sins. And multiply by his
stitches.*

Hilary is coming next Friday.

Sincerely but confused, Laura

Lorinda stretched before getting out of bed.
Out the window she could see the village kids
trooping off to Black Pond with their skates. I'd
go now too, she thought, but Hilary's arriving on
Friday, and I can't wait to meet her.

6

Lorinda turned over on her stomach and propped the diary up on the bed. Then she started to read the new entry.

Dear Diary: Today Hilary arrived. There was a knock at the door and I answered it. And there she was. There's a lady in charge of Guest Children, and she brought her. Nobody was supposed to know when Hilary's ship arrived, so we had to just stay home and pretend that nothing special was happening. She's not one bit like I expected. In fact, it's really hard to know what to say about her. But I'll try.

First of all, she looks really young. I look centuries older than her. She's real little, and she has these long, long pigtails that she must have been growing ever since the very minute she was born. She has a round face and big metal-rimmed glasses — round like her face. She looks about as old as Eric.

But wait'll you hear this, Diary. When she opens her mouth and speaks, she sounds like she's about thirty-five. Very lah-dee-dah. "I was most fearfully cold on the ship," she said. "What a mercy I'd taken along my jumper." Jumper! "What's a jumper?" I asked. "You've one on at the moment," she said, pointing to my sweater. I said, "Well, we call them — " but my mother interrupted. "Upstairs, you two," she said, in a loud voice. "Let's take Hilary's things up to her room."

So we did. I opened the door and stood back, like it was a picture I'd painted or a piece of giant sculpture. My creation. "We fixed it all up for you," I said. "Look at the mauve rug. Ever nice, eh?"

She stood at the doorway, holding her suitcase in front of her, and looked all around. Then she said, "Jolly pretty. Thank you for being so kind."

I thought, good grief, how am I ever going to have a conversation with this kid? What'll we talk about? I'd probably have to discuss the international situation or poetry or something.

Then, dear Diary, what a shock. When she was unpacking, I could see that she had a doll in her suitcase. She tried really fast to put a sweater — a jumper — on top of it, but I saw it. I said, "Hey. You've got a doll." "Yes," she said. She picked it up and clasped it to her chest, covering it with both her arms, like I was going to kill it, or something. So I said, real quick, "She looks nice. Does she have a name?" And Hilary gave me such a look as I can't describe — sort of desperate, like a hunted animal. And she said, "Yes. Her name is Agatha." And I said, "It's a lovely name," although I thought it was a hideous name. But I was hoping that the hunted look might go away. There she was, standing on the mauve rug, with her funny navy blue hat on (with a brim) and a little navy blue coat with a belt, hugging Agatha like the two of them were all alone in the world.

Suddenly my mother said, "When you're unpacked, come on down and have some bread and peanut butter. You two can get acquainted while I work on supper." And then she left.

I said, "Do you want a crib for Agatha? I bet there's one up in the attic."

She sighed and said, "No thank you. I

think I want her on my bed." Then she said, "Mummy told me there'd be peanut butter."

I thought this was a pretty funny thing for her to say. So I said, "How come?"

She said, "How come?"

I said, "Yes. How come? Why did she say that? Don't you have peanut butter in England?"

"No," she said.

"Why?" I asked.

"I don't want to say," she said, hat still on, coat still done up.

"Say," I ordered.

"Mummy said it was because no one likes it. They do have little jars of it in the shops for the Americans when they come over in the summer. Mummy says Americans think that life can't be carried on without peanut butter, so we make just enough for the tourists."

I laughed. "Canadians, too," I said. "Better make some more." Then I added, "Maybe you'll like it."

"I very much doubt I shall," she said, "if the entire nation finds it unpleasant. But I shall try. Mummy says — said — I was to try everything and be cheerful at all times."

I wasn't sure what to do with this kid.

When she started talking like a thirty-five year old, I felt clumsy and stupid and <u>young</u>. When I looked at her with that doll, I felt like her grandmother. It was very confusing. I didn't know whether she needed to be protected or slapped down to size.

I decided to try protection.

"Can I help you unpack?" I asked. She didn't seem to have very much stuff — just two big suitcases for summer and winter and for maybe years and years.

Years and years. Suddenly I hoped the war would hurry up and be over. I wasn't sure I wanted this peculiar girl in my house for years and years.

"I can do it," she said.

"Why don't you take your coat off?" I asked.

Then down went the doll on the bed, and off came the navy blue coat and the bowler hat.

She had a funny little tunic on underneath.

"What grade are you in, in school?" I said.

"We don't have grades at my school. We have forms. And they're different. So I don't know."

"Well," I said, "probably you'll be in the same class as me."

"I do hope so," she said, sitting on the edge of the bed with her hands in her lap, rubbing her thumbs together. Then she said, "Is it always this hot in your houses?"

It didn't seem hot to me. But I could remember my dad saying, "If you go to someone's house for dinner in England, you nearly freeze to death."

"My dad says you don't have central heating. No furnaces and stuff."

"No. We have lovely cheerful fireplaces."

"Well," I said, "turn off the radiator if you're too hot. I'll show you how." I showed her.

Then I said, "Would you like to unpack by yourself?"

And she said, "Yes, thank you. I'd prefer that." Which I can certainly understand, if all her clothes are as weird as the ones she had on.

Now it's nine p.m. and she's in bed. I hope I can find some kind of key to open her up. She's not like anything I ever met before in my whole life. Mother says that's because all countries have customs that are different — different clothes, voices, education, songs, games. She said to be pa-

*tient. She said I'd get used to her and she'd
get used to me. Then, just as I was starting
to feel really friendly towards Mother —
like we were getting close to each other —
she said, "Your room's a mess. Go clear it
up before supper." And then I felt mad
again. I'm glad I have Eileen. Even if
Mother and Hilary let me down, I know I
can always depend on Eileen.*

*I'm sitting here in bed — thinking how
strange we all must seem to Hilary. Maybe
even scary. The only familiar thing in her
life right now is that old rag doll, Agatha.*

*She didn't like the peanut butter. I felt
myself getting really cross about that. I
thought, you just decided you weren't going
to like it. You didn't even give it half a
chance. You're just tagging along behind
your entire nation.*

In dire confusion, Laura

Lorinda stopped reading and looked up at the
ceiling. "Oh, Grandma," she whispered, "stay nice
to her, even if she's a bit of a nerd." She was
remembering the first terrible weeks at Aunt
Marion's, when she and James had been all alone
in the new world of Ontario. She remembered
Mildred making fun of her Nova Scotia accent,

63

her clothes, the way she called her mother Mummy. What next, she wondered?

Dear Diary: I guess I didn't mention it, but yesterday when Hilary arrived, she wasn't alone. A whole shipment of Guest Children landed in Halifax. I said this to Dad, and he said I made them sound like potatoes or doughnuts or something. Was it ever smart to bring them in on a Friday afternoon. That gives us a chance to get used to them over the weekend, before we have to face a huge army of them in school on Monday.

I forgot to tell you, but Eileen's got one, too. Her name is Judith Ramsay-Davis. Yes, Ramsay-Davis. Eileen says she talks about cricket all the time. It's some kind of game. Norman said what did we expect her to talk about — hockey? And that they come from a country where they think cricket is the most important thing in the world.

We went over — Hilary and I — to Eileen's in the afternoon and met Judith. Hilary hadn't met her on the boat, and I knew she was excited and full of hope, although she doesn't exactly tell you what she's thinking. You have to guess. But right away I knew it wasn't working between them. Hilary's thumbs were rubbing, rubbing, and she was looking maybe even more frantic than yesterday. If I'd thought Hilary sounded lah-dee-dah, I have to tell you, dear Diary, that Judith sounded like a duchess or a queen or something. On the way home, I said to Hilary, "You didn't talk much to Judith. How come?"

Hilary gave me a long hard look. Then she said, "I don't think you'd understand."

"Try me," I said. "Come on. Open up, kiddo."

"Well . . ."

"Come on, come on," I said.

"Mummy said that Canadians aren't divided up into different classes the same way we are in England."

"Classes! What do you mean? Like in school?" This kid could go miles around a subject before she got to the point. But do you think she answered that one right off? No. Listen to what she said.

"Judith's father's a lawyer. She doesn't speak like I do. Didn't you notice? She goes to Rhodeen — one of the poshest schools in England. I go to St. Jerome's. My father's a clerk in a furniture shop. Except right now," and as she said this, her voice sort of cracked, "he's a pilot." Then she added, "That's what I mean by different classes."

I got mad at this. "So your dad's a pilot," I said, "defending your country. Who cares if Mr. Ramsay-Whatsit is the king's brother! What on earth could be better than a pilot?"

I looked at Hilary, and her eyes were so wet and full of juice that you could hardly see the pupils. But she took two long quavery breaths and said, "Some people say the war may change all the class distinctions. They say that fighting side by side will make people feel like brothers. And sisters. That after a while, no one will care who's lower class and who's upper class. But Mummy says that that kind of thing runs deeper and stronger than any war."

Then she brushed her forehead with her hand in a kind of tired way and said, "I think I'll go in my room now and be alone for a while."

So when we got home, that's what she did. I wanted to kill Judith for making Hilary feel like that. But when I told this to Dad, he said, "What exactly did Judith do?"

I thought, and then I said, "Nothing. She just talked about the boat trip and asked Hilary how she was getting along. I guess *she didn't do anything wrong at all."*

"Exactly," said Dad. "Hilary's mother was right. That feeling runs so deep that it'll take more than a war to destroy it. Remember — this isn't the only war. The last one didn't change much of anything. It's just as hard to be chummy with a duchess in the 1940s as it was in 1918."

This made me feel really discouraged, and I was glad Hilary hadn't heard what he said. I felt like I was Hilary's mother — frantically trying to protect her. And powerless to help.

Distressed,
Laura

Lorinda could hardly wait to read the next entry. By now, she'd lost track of time, and she wouldn't have left the diary if there'd been six rinks in her front yard.

7

Dear Diary: I'm dying to tell you about today. I feel like I'm living in a whole new world. And I guess I am. This is Monday, and our first day at school with the new shipment of English Guest Children. Ours is a really small school, with kindergarten to high school right on the same grounds, so when you dump twenty-five English guest kids into it, you know they're there.

And suddenly Hilary doesn't look so strange. She just sort of looks like everyone else's sister. The girls all seem to have those really simple coats with belts, like little tiny kids would wear, and straight hair with a bobby pin or else pigtails. And a lot of them wear those funny hats. They all have accents, but there seem to be a bunch of different ones. Hilary isn't looking so *tense today. You can see she knows she isn't alone any more.*

They're going to give the new kids a bunch of tests this afternoon. To see where they fit. I hope Hilary is in grade 7 with me. She may still need some looking after. Even if she's one of twenty-five, it can't be easy to look nine years old when you're thirteen.

Eileen is acting kind of funny. Like she seems to be stuck to Judith like glue. And when I dashed up to her at recess to unload a whole lot of succulent secrets, she just waved her hand <u>airily</u> and said, "Oh, hi!" and then turned back to talk to a couple of the new kids. (By the way, they don't have KIDS in England. They have girls and boys and children and chums.) When Judith handed Eileen an apple, I heard Eileen say, "Oh! Jolly good!" <u>Eileen</u>. I wanted to kill her. From the English kids, that stuff is starting to sound almost normal. Coming from Eileen, it sounded disgusting.

Lorinda put down the diary in a rage. That Eileen, she thought. At least Duncan's not a traitor, even if he does boss me around. She looked at the clock: 10:30. Still time to get in a little skating before lunch. She tossed the diary to the bottom of the bed and raced downstairs.

"What's up?" asked her mother.

"Going skating," mumbled Lorinda as she fished around among the books and rubbers to find her skates. "Gotta hurry. I'm late."

"Oh, Lorinda," sighed her mother. "Are you sure it's safe? There was a thaw while we were away, you know."

"Mom!" Lorinda looked up from the floor, a frown between her eyebrows. "Of *course* it's safe. It was minus twenty yesterday. I wish you didn't worry about *everything*!"

"Sometimes I can't help it," said Mrs. Dauphinee. "My oldest brother went through the ice when we were kids. I never told you before."

"What happened?" Lorinda was standing up now, skates in hand.

"He drowned," said her mother, her voice small and unsteady.

Lorinda's fist flew to her mouth. "Mom! Oh no! But why? Couldn't anyone fish him out?"

"It was a big lake. And he was a daredevil. He kept skating near the edge of the open water just to make the girls squeal. When he went in, he got caught under the ice and no one could find him." Then she added, "I was there . . . and saw everything."

"*Grandma's* son?"

Mrs. Dauphinee gave a nervous laugh. "Of course Grandma's son. He was my brother, for goodness sake."

Lorinda sat down on a kitchen chair, skates hanging between her knees. "Oh, poor Grandma. She's such a sensitive person."

"*Is* such a sensitive person, Lorinda?"

Lorinda sighed. "Yes. *Is.* I can't bear to think of how awful that must have been for her. And for you, too, Mom, honest." Lorinda sat still and stared into space for a few moments. Then she got up slowly and started to put on her jacket and mitts.

"Look, Mom," she said, touching her mother's arm. "I'm real sorry about your brother. Real sorry. But listen. It's okay. Black Lake is just a small lake. And there aren't any open places at all. And no funny currents. Don't worry."

"I'll try," said her mother. "But remember. I happen to be a sensitive person, too."

Lorinda stopped fiddling with her zipper for a moment, and gazed at her mother with a long look. Then she grinned, and gave her a little squeeze. "I guess you are, at that," she said. Then she was out the door, slamming it behind her.

Down at Black Lake, the ice was still almost perfect, and it seemed as though everyone Lorinda knew was there — George, Glynis,

Fiona, even Reginald Corkum. And Duncan. He shouted a loud "Hi!" to her, and came rushing over, jumping over cracks and sometimes skating backwards. Showing off, thought Lorinda. But nice. Doesn't hold a grudge. Always there. Loyal.

Lorinda sped over to meet him, and they skated off together, keeping in step, moving in unison.

That night, as soon as she'd finished her homework, Lorinda raced upstairs to open the diary.

Dear Diary, (she read) *They did all their testing of the English kids, and guess what? They all know ten times more than we do, so they're pushing them all ahead one or two grades. Hilary's in grade 10. She's in the same class as Gloria Holton, who wears greasy lipstick and is all the time patting her hair. Poor Hilary.*

We've got two of the kids in our class and they're only eleven years old. Judith's in grade 9. So maybe Eileen will be forced to realize that I'm still alive. I guess the English school system must be miles ahead of ours. I can't believe how much these kids know — especially about things like literature and French.

Suddenly I feel so dumb. And so sort of <u>flimsy</u>. I found myself wishing today that I had one of those funny navy blue coats *with the belts. I felt like I wanted to be one of them. My gosh — I felt like an <u>outsider</u>. And it's my school and my country! But right now, the whole school's revolving around those kids. They're special, and I feel like a great big nothing.*

I talked to Dad about all that stuff, and he said to just be patient. "It'll all sort itself out," he said. "By the end of a couple of months or years, you'll all be richer for having known one another."

I think that being in the war was what made Dad so patient. I think maybe he figured that since he got out of it alive, with just a limp, he wasn't going to worry about anything else — except <u>really</u> big things — for the rest of his life. But I haven't been in a war like him. I'm not that patient.

Impatiently, Laura

So, thought Lorinda, who had taken time out to run a bath, that's where Mom gets all that worry stuff. And it seems like James is a bit like Norman.

She poured her birthday bubble bath into the tub and swished the water around till the bubbles got high and stiff. Amazing, she thought, how people pass things along to their children. Will I be a worry-wart too? Maybe if you know there's something like that floating around in your system, you can fight it — make it not happen. Otherwise it might just creep up and take over, without you really noticing.

When Lorinda got back to her room, Jessie was sound asleep in her little iron bed, snoring a small, soft, gurgly snore that was almost comforting. Lorinda dived into bed, propped up the pillows, and started reading again.

Dear Diary: Sorry not to have written for so long.

We all have to put big heavy black curtains over our windows, and Mother is sewing hard all the time to get some made. Black-out curtains, they're called. So the enemy submarines won't see our ships silhouetted against the light, and torpedo them. It's a huge job, but the air raid wardens say everyone has to have them. Otherwise we can't turn on the lights when it's dark. And we're forever testing our air raid sirens. At night, there are planes up in the sky, and they try to find them with searchlights. It's a little bit scary, but exciting too.

Gillian is one of the Guest Children in my class. She's only eleven, but this doesn't stop her from acting like we're all a lot of stupid dopes. She says that our war stuff is just play-acting, and that here in Canada we don't even know what a war is. Maybe that's true, but I sure wish she'd shut up about it.

When we were playing ground hockey yesterday, I had this awful urge to hit her in the shins. (But I didn't.) She says we're second-rate hockey players. I guess she's right, because those kids seem to be better than we are in sports as well as everything else. But I think it's _repulsive_ to be forever saying your own country is better than someone else's. I'm waiting impatiently for the day when Gillian tries to stand up on a pair of skates. I'm just going to stand there and smile in a very superior way and say, "Could I be of some assistance to you, Gillian?" It will _kill_ her to ask for my help.

You can't believe how one bunch of kids can be so different from another bunch, even though they're all the same age and everyone speaks English. But sometimes the English we all speak is miles apart. They don't say "Hi" like we do. I don't know how they get along without such a useful word. They say "Hello." They use the word "sweets" instead of "candy." We say "Right!" They say "Right-O!" And cookies are biscuits.

What else is different? One thing is snow. The first day it snowed, they acted like they were in a kind of North Pole Heaven. It was an early snowstorm, but there was a lot of it, and by the next day, everything was about five or six inches deep in snow. The English kids just rushed out and rolled around in it, without stopping to put on any boots or mittens. They were that excited. Snow doesn't come very often to the southern parts of England (almost never) and when it does, it's an _event_.

This business of being different is hard on everyone. I found Hilary one day in front of the mirror, holding up her long hair so that it looked short, and beside her on the sink was a pair of scissors. She said, "I want to cut it. So I'll look like other people. But . . ."

"But what?" I said.

"But Mummy really loved it. My long hair."

I didn't know what to say to that. So I just picked up the scissors and put them away.

The kids — Hilary and Judith and Gillian and the rest of them — talk a lot about the terrible dangers in England. About being down in air raid shelters and fearing for their lives. About hearing the bombs screaming out of the sky and then landing with a terrible boom. About the fires they've seen all over their towns at night. I'm ashamed, but when I hear all that, I feel inferior again, and wish we could have a few of those things happen to us, so I'd feel even.

Dad almost never gets mad, but when I said that to him, he said, "Don't let me ever again hear you say such a stupid thing. You don't know what you're talking about." Then that made me mad, and I said, "If I don't know what I'm talking about, it's your fault, because you always refuse to talk about the First World War."

Then Dad got very white, and he stood up, almost as though he wanted to be higher than me when he spoke. He just looked at me for a few moments and his face kind of dragged down like there were weights on it. Then he said,

"War is a lot of things, but one thing it isn't is _romantic_. So get that out of your head. It often means the kind of pain that makes men scream, and fear that puts such *knots inside you that you can't eat or sleep. And it's dirt and terrible smells and death to the left and the right and in front and behind. And it's burns and mutilation and blindness and sorrow and a terrible anguished realization of the waste of human lives."*

Of course, I could think of nothing to say to that, so there was a silence. Then he said, "I never said that to you before, because I didn't want to scare you. But it seems to me that you're sort of playing with this war, and making light of what those kids have suffered. I guess if they can go through it, you can at least put up with hearing about it."

"I'll get you some coffee," I said to him, and went out to the kitchen to heat water. Honest to goodness, Diary, it's the only thing I could think of to say.

Yours, clobbered, Laura

Lorinda stopped reading and looked out the dark window towards the hills on the other side of the Bay. Beyond those hills, she knew, was Halifax. She thought about the huge explosion in Halifax in the First World War. Over 1,900 people had been killed, and 9,000 more wounded; it had even blinded 199. She thought about Grandma's father's experiences in that same war — too terrible to talk about. And she thought about people crowded into air raid shelters in the last war, wondering if the whistling bombs would land on their own houses — or on them. And, like Laura, like Grandma, she felt ashamed.

How could I ever have thought of those wars as "little shooting wars," she thought. Nuclear weapons were unthinkably terrible, she knew, but even a bow and arrow can kill you or blind you. And dead is dead. And blindness is blindness.

Carefully she put the diary under her bed and turned off the light. In her dream that night, she and Grandma, she and Laura, were down in an air raid shelter, and they were crying as they heard bomb after bomb land on the city. When the all-clear siren sounded — the long steady whine that tells you that all the enemy planes have left — she sat bolt upright in her bed. But it was just her alarm clock ringing; so she reached over to shut it off.

8

As Lorinda continued to read the diary, she felt more and more as though she knew her grandmother and her friends, the Guest Children. She didn't read as much or as quickly as she had planned. The diary was too long. Besides, she wanted it to last and last. She felt as though she were living in two worlds — her own, and another one, long ago in the 1940s, when her grandmother had been so young. But getting older, thought Lorinda.

One morning, she awoke long before it was light, and dived under her covers with a flashlight to read the latest entry.

Dear Diary: The most important thing I have to tell you today is that I met Judith's cousin this morning. He's going to another school. His name is Ian, which I think is a wonderful name — sort of clipped and dignified and mature. Like he is. You should see him, dear Diary. He's got all this blond hair that grows on his head in such a classy way. He's got kind of a broad face with amazing cheek-bones, and a big smile with dazzling white teeth. He is very poised. He doesn't fidget or bite his nails or keep staring at a point behind your head.

Mostly, I sort of hate boys, so it was a shock to meet Ian. Boys of thirteen or fourteen usually are so silly, screaming and yelling and seeing how far they can spit, and going around puffing out their chests, and practising their new deep voices — if they happen to have them. And they never seem to come any higher than my shoulder, which makes me feel like a giant, or one of nature's mistakes, or something. Plus I never know what to say to them. Sometimes I want to impress them and make them notice me. Other times I want to give them a kick and say, "Out of my way, dopes."

But it's like Ian came from another planet, he's that different. He's tall for his age, for one thing, and he's not so darned pushy. He just sort of _is_. He's fourteen and he's in grade 11. When he sits down, he doesn't sit on the edge of the chair and jiggle the change in his pockets, like all the other boys. He sits back, very relaxed, and sticks one leg on top of his other knee — at right angles to it. Like you'd expect Cary Grant to sit, or David Niven. Then, instead of silly jokes, he talks about England and the war. He says it all in a matter-of-fact way, but he makes me able to see the fires burning and hear the bombs whistling.

I asked if his father was in the army or navy or anything. He said he was too old to be out shooting things but that he had a desk job in the army. I said, what was that? A desk job, I mean. He said it had to do with intelligence. That seemed a funny thing to say. Of <u>course</u> Ian's father would be intelligent, but you don't talk about it. That's boasting — something I can't stand. I was disappointed in Ian, who I had thought was nearly perfect. Then I asked Mother the next day, and she said Intelligence had to do with discovering enemy secrets and manoovers (whatever that means). (I just looked it up in the dictionary and you spell it *MANOEUVRES*). And I thought, oh my gosh, Ian's father is a sort of Master Spy. If I end up a spy, I could be working for him.

Before I go to sleep tonight, I'm going to work up a really delicious daydream about me in a beige raincoat coming in to discuss my case with Ian's father. He will be tall and look exactly like Ian, but old and tanned, with lines in his face. He'll say, "Jolly good job, Laura. Absolutely topping. Without your contribution, we might never have been able to save London." Just then, Ian will come in, grown up and way over six feet tall, and will take me by the arm and say, "Come along, Laura. The plane for France is leaving in ten minutes. The Underground will be on hand to meet you."

When people say the Underground I still (in my head) see tunnels under the earth. I do this even though Ian has explained to me that the Underground is the name used for people who help our armies in secret ways in countries occupied by the Nazis. They hide spies and things like that. And help Jews get out of the country, because Nazis do terrible things to Jews, who never even did a single thing to deserve it. Ian says that he's heard the Nazis want everyone to be blond and tall, with pure unpolluted blood, and that they figure if they rule the world they can maybe make that happen. I won't have a chance because I have jet black hair and dark brown eyes.

Norman says he doesn't believe in war and that it's a stupid and evil way for people to try to solve their problems. I said, "Then how come you're going to join up when you're eighteen, which is only one month away?"

He said, "Shh! Mother'll hear. She's in the kitchen." Then he said, "Because this is an unusual war. You can't let people go swallow up Europe and then maybe North America, and kill off all the Jews and be rulers of everybody else, and make everyone be blond and tall and think the same way. The Nazis believe in bad things, and if they ruled us, when we had kids, the kids would start believing bad things too."

I said, "Why are they specially mean to Jews?" And he said he wasn't sure, but maybe the Nazis didn't like it that many of the Jews were extra clever and also some of them were rich, and ran successful businesses and were big wheels in universities. If the Nazis were going to be the Master Race, they didn't want any people around who were perhaps smarter and richer than they were. Anyway, he said that's why he had to go to war.

I said, "Aren't you scared?"

He said, "Yes." Then he said, "<u>Very</u>."

It was terrible when he said "Very." It made all my daydreams about being proud when his ship sails out the harbour seem silly, almost mean. All I can think of now is that he's going to do something he thinks he has to do, and that it scares the daylights out of him.

I thought of the things Dad told me about war. The wounding and blinding and fear and smells and dying. And I understand why Dad can't bear to talk about it. I can hardly stand to write about it. Because now, even to me, it seems real. It's not like just an exciting story any more.

Scared, Laura

That morning when Lorinda put away the diary, she felt sad and tired in a way she'd never felt before. Then she thought, do I feel about Duncan the way Laura — Grandma — is starting to feel about Ian? No. She didn't. Duncan had been her best friend since she was a little kid, and he just seemed ordinary — but of course special, in the way a best friend always is.

Then she thought about Sarah Cohen, who'd been her best friend in Peterborough. She was Jewish. Lorinda found herself wondering about Sarah's grandparents. She knew that her grandfather and her great aunt had come to Canada from Holland at the end of the war. She remembered Sarah saying, "They came alone, because that was all that was left of the family." At the time, Lorinda just thought the rest of them had maybe gone somewhere else, or that there'd been a flu epidemic or something. Now, with a stab of horror, she wondered if she knew what Sarah had really meant.

Lorinda had planned to catch a little more sleep before getting up, but just thinking about Sarah's family made her feel as though her eyes were glued open. So she got out the diary and read one more entry.

Dear Diary: Today one good thing happened and one bad thing.

The good thing was that Geoffrey came to Sunday tea. Geoffrey is in the navy, and he visits our house every time his ship comes into Halifax. The city is so spilling over with people that often the servicemen and women have no place to go when they get leave. The restaurants and theatres are all full, and sometimes it seems like Halifax is just one big long line-up. But lots of the people in the forces have sort of foster homes with families in our city and in Dartmouth.

On Sundays, we have dinner at noon,

and then we have tea about five o'clock. This week we made sandwiches and cut up celery and had those yummy chocolate cupcakes with frosting on top and whipped cream in the centre. We almost never have them any more, because sugar is rationed. Heaven will have those cupcakes stacked up on shelves from one side to the other. Of heaven, I mean.

Lots of servicemen come to our house, but Geoffrey is my favourite. He's not an officer, so he wears a sailor suit with bell-bottom trousers and a tight top with a sailor collar. He always comes in without knocking, because we gave him a key, and Mother says he's just like a third son, and Geoffrey calls her Mom. He always runs upstairs after yelling "Hi!," and right away we can hear the water running in the tub. He says when the war's over, he's going to spend the rest of his life in the bathtub.

Well, Geoffrey and Hilary really hit it off. He's relaxed and funny and fun, and before long, even stiff old Hilary (who I really love, but gee whiz I wish she'd loosen up) was doubled up laughing. Then he said, "I've been in England right near where you live." And her eyes opened up really wide, and she went over and sat be-

side him and even touched his arm. Those
eyes looked like they were going to jump
right out of her head. She whispered, "Tell
me about it." So he did.

He said it was beautiful, with tidy fields
and high hedges. He said you could see the
English Channel from some of the hills
and that the air was "soft and fresh and
damp." That's what he said — soft and
fresh and damp. I want to be an author
some day, so I rushed out to the kitchen
and wrote that down on our grocery list on
the fridge.

The more Geoffrey talked, the more questions Hilary asked, and it was like she
came alive all over her prim, stiff little
body. She waved her arms around, and her
pigtails were flying, and her eyes were
bright and happy behind her round glasses.
I felt guilty that sometimes she makes me
mad because she's such a stick, and I
wished I knew how to get her all zapped up
like that. Then we had tea, and Geoffrey
went back to his ship.

The bad thing is that at bedtime, I came
out of the bathroom and passed Hilary's
room. Behind her closed door I could hear
awful sounds, like someone was stran-
gling. And I knew what it was. It was Hil-

ary crying and trying to do it so no one would hear.

I wanted to comfort her, but I didn't know how. Besides, I knew she wouldn't want me to see her like that. So I went and got Mother. She went in, and I sat on the stairway and waited and listened. I could hear Mother's murmuring voice, and I knew she was doing whatever she could to make Hilary feel better. Mother is very tidy and clean, but she's super good at comforting, and when she hugs you, you feel safe and warm and looked after. But when she came out of Hilary's room, there was a worry-line between her eyebrows, and she said, "I can't break through. I can't seem to help her. She's like a piece of granite rock. Those British . . ." she sighed.

"Those British?" I asked.

"So darned brave and stiff-upper-lipped that no one can get near them. She just breaks my heart. She's just a little girl, and she's trying to act like a heroine of thirty-five." She sighed again, kissed me on the top of my head, and went downstairs.

Now I'm in bed, and it's like everything in me is sad or mad. I'm sad for Hilary and even for Mother who wants to help her and can't. And I'm mad at Hitler and the

war and at all the unnecessary things that
make people unhappy.

Sad, Laura

Well, thought Lorinda, as she put the diary on
her night table and switched off her flashlight, *that*
certainly didn't cheer me up any. It was still dark,
but she grabbed her clothes and tiptoed down to
the kitchen to put them on where it was warm.
She took the diary with her, so she could read
some more in the rocking chair beside the warm
oil stove.

9

It had snowed during the night, and everything looked white and clean in Blue Harbour in the growing dawn. Even the piles of old wooden boxes and the coils of tarred rope wore caps of snow, and the spruce trees behind the houses looked like something on a Christmas card.

Thank heavens I don't live in a city, thought Lorinda, as she hauled on her jeans. Even though Laura seems to like Halifax, I think I'd die if I had to live in the middle of all that traffic, without the sea there to greet me every morning. It would be like dying of thirst. Of course, you could climb up on Citadel Hill and look right out to sea; she knew that from her trip there with Hank and James and Mildred. But a person couldn't be forever and ever climbing up and down the Citadel.

She remembered the wide, wide mouth of Halifax Harbour, and recalled her father telling her that during the last war, there'd been a long gate that reached right down to the sea bottom suspended across it — to keep out enemy ships and submarines. She shivered, and wondered if Grandma had known about that. Imagine making a gate that huge!

While she waited for the rest of the family to wake up, Lorinda curled up by the stove and read another entry from the diary. I'd like something *nice* to happen before I start my day, she thought.

> *Dear Diary: Tomorrow is Norman's birthday. Eric is all excited about it, and keeps jumping around like a flea, saying, "Shh! Shh! I know something about you!" and poking his finger at Norman.*
>
> *Eric is just hepped up because there'll be a big cake with those great decorations Mother puts on top. Coloured stuff sprinkled on, and candy roses. Mother always saves up sugar ration stamps so that birthday cakes can be wickedly sweet, with four layers and lots of frosting, and goo between the layers. Norman's girlfriend is coming for supper and his best friend, Harry. But Norman is very quiet today, and when Eric jumps around being a nuisance, he just smiles sadly and follows him with his eyes.*
>
> *I know what he's thinking. He's thinking that when he's out there tossing around on*

the angry winter seas, watching for sub-
marines that could blow him to bits any
minute, even the memory of Eric may look
good. This is hard to imagine, but no doubt
it's true. Me, I can't think of any situation
that would make Eric look good.

And of course Norman is wondering how
to tell Mother and Dad about joining the
navy. Boy oh boy! Some birthday!

Yours, Laura

There was a sound at the door, and Lorinda looked up to see James enter the kitchen. Good old James, she thought. He drives me bonkers sometimes because he's so doggone calm, but he sure is a big improvement over Eric. She wished she could put Norman and James in the same room and let them talk to each other. James was only ten, but he'd be right at home with Norman. They both sort of *knew* things — the kind of things she'd started to discover, now that she was thirteen. But it was as though James had been *born* knowing them. Sometimes she thought he could see right inside her skin.

"Hi," he said, putting his glasses on.

"If there's a war," said Lorinda, "you won't be able to go."

"Huh?" muttered James, shaking bran flakes into a bowl.

"Because of your awful eyes. Thank goodness."

"War?" said James.

"Yes," answered Lorinda. "I'm living through World War II right now, and I'm really worried about that family. In the diary, Grandma's brother is going to war any minute, and it's going to be *awful*."

James thought about that.

"Tell me more," he said.

So Lorinda did. While the sun came up over Pony Island, she told him the whole story — about Grandma's silent father and his feelings about war, about her tidy but warmhearted mother, about Eric and Norman, about Hilary, about the Guest Children, about the war.

"Well," said James. "I know what Norman *won't* do."

"What?"

"He won't spoil that birthday, or the cake that was made with all those ration stamps. He'll wait till the next day. If it was me . . ." He paused.

"If it was?"

"I'd tell them the *next* day that I was going to do it — and I'd tell them *before* I did it."

"Why?"

"If you hear about something after it's happened, you feel, well, sort of trapped."

"Well, they're gonna be trapped anyway. If you enlist, you can't unenlist."

"I know that. But if you hear about it afterwards, you keep thinking that maybe you could have stopped it. Or his mom and dad might think maybe they could have got him to wait six more months in case the war was over by then."

"But it *wasn't* over by then. It went on till 1945. I know. I looked it up." Lorinda cut up a banana and put the pieces on top of her peanut butter sandwich.

"Okay. But that's not what I'm talking about. I'm talking about what his parents will *think* when he tells them. And what if he gets killed two months after he joins up? They'll be forever and ever sad that they hadn't held him back a little longer."

Lorinda was staring. "Norman? *Killed?*"

James shrugged his shoulders. "I'm sorry, Lorinda," he said. "But he *could* be, you know."

Lorinda stood up. "I know what I'll do," she said. "I'll ask Mom if he got back from the war okay. She'll know. I hear her talking to Jessie upstairs." She started out of the kitchen, and then James spoke again.

"If I was you, I wouldn't."

"Why, for pete's sake?"

"Well, you're reading that diary like it was twenty times better than those detective books you're always buried in. D'you want to know the ending *now*? And how'll you feel the day Norman enlists if you know he dies or goes blind or loses his legs or something?"

Lorinda sat down, suddenly too weak to stand up any longer. She covered her face with her hands for a moment, then dropped them limp into her lap. "You're right, James," she sighed. "This is bad enough to be living through without having a crystal ball to see into the future." Then she sprang out of her chair again. "Hey!" she cried. "There's Duncan and Fiona. And George and Glynis. With toboggans."

Duncan was already in the back porch. "Get moving!" he was shouting. "Get your clothes on and dig your toboggan out of the barn! We're going tobogganing!"

Lorinda sighed. "Duncan," she said, when he came into the kitchen, snowy boots and all, "could you maybe once, just once, *ask* me to do something instead of *ordering* me to do it? Just once?"

Duncan frowned. "Why? What's the problem? There's a lot of snow. Good snow — not sticky. Of course you're coming tobogganing. What's all the fuss about?"

Lorinda sat firmly on the chair and folded her arms. "Duncan," she said, "you're my best friend, so try to do what I ask. It isn't very hard, and maybe you could get used to it and even like it."

"What? Sure. Whadda you want?"

"Please. Repeat after me. Lorinda, how'd you like to go tobogganing today?"

"Gimme a break, Lorinda! Don't be so stupid!"

Lorinda looked at him hard, and didn't move.

"Duncan," she said, "unlike some people I could mention, I'm not telling you. I'm asking you. Try it. It won't kill you. 'Lorinda, how'd you like to go tobogganing today?' "

Duncan's red eyebrows came down over his eyes and almost met each other above his nose. "Silly darn girl stuff!" he growled.

Lorinda sat there, face blank, icy calm. "I could write it down for you," she said, "if you don't remember the words."

Duncan half turned, and fiddled with the door knob, as though trying to decide whether or not to leave.

"The words are — " began Lorinda.

"I heard you!" yelled Duncan. There was a long silent pause, and you could tell that even upstairs, everyone was listening. Then Duncan said, as fast as a machine gun, "Lorinda-how'd-you-like-to-go-tobogganing-today?"

Lorinda rose from her chair and smiled very, very sweetly. "Why, Duncan! What a neat idea! I'll just get my warm clothes on real fast, because I don't want to keep you waiting."

A little pigtailed face peeked around the back

door. It was Glynis. "Hi!" she cried to everybody. "Is it ever nice out! James, how'd you like to go tobogganing today?"

Duncan stared at the ceiling and hit the side of his head with the flat of his hand. "I don't believe it!" he groaned. Then suddenly everyone burst out laughing — everyone, that is, except Glynis, who had no idea what all the fuss was about.

Just before Lorinda turned her light out that evening, she opened the diary to the day of Norman's birthday. This time Laura had dated it.

Date: June 28

Dear Diary: This day was so long, I can't believe it. Mother and I had fun fixing Norman's cake, even though she kept telling me to clean up the stuff I spilled and to pile the dishes and keep the knife clean. I wish she wouldn't! But it was fun anyway, because she let me decorate the top — the most important part, I think. But all the time, I kept thinking, no one is going to want to eat this cake when they hear what Norman has to tell them. They'll never want to decorate or eat another cake as long as they live.

In the afternoon, Norman and his girl-

friend Alice went for a long, long walk.
When they got back, I could tell by her face
that he hadn't told her. She just looked
happy and sort of electric. She's wildly in
love with Norman. But I don't know if he's
as wild as she is. When he's with her, he
doesn't act like he's beside himself with
passion.

Before supper, Norman and I talked up
in the attic, while Mother cooked the meal
and Alice went home to put on her best
dress. It seemed like it was the only place
we could be private. I said, "How can you
stand telling them?"

"Today?" he said, surprised. "You don't
think I'm going to tell them _today_! Do you
think I'm crazy? I'm going to enlist day
after tomorrow. Tomorrow I'll tell them.
All of them. Alice, too."

"Wait'll she sees you in a sailor suit," I
said.

He grinned. "That's the only thing about
this whole business that I'm looking forward to."

I gave him a big hug, and he held me a
lot tighter and longer than usual. Then we
went down to the party. Hilary gave him
a little book about England. Inside, it said,
"Thank you for being like a brother to me."

*That's a pretty opened-up thing for Hilary
to say. He got a lot of presents — a fishing
rod, stamps for his collection from Harry,
theatre tickets, stuff like that. I looked at
them all and thought, I bet the only present
that he'll get any use out of is Hilary's.*

I'm sleepy, so I'm going to stop.

ZZZZZZZ, Laura

Lorinda sighed. I don't think I can stand the
suspense, she thought, but I can't stay awake another minute. She fell asleep before she turned
out the light.

10

Lorinda stood inside the little shelter, waiting for the school bus. She had found a small empty space way back in the corner, and she was reading Grandma's diary. If I don't, she had thought before leaving the house, I think I'll just have to stay home today. I can't survive if I don't know what happens when Norman makes his big announcement.

"Look! Look! Everybody, look!
Look at Lorinda
With her nose in a book!"

This was Reginald Corkum, but it was a friendly chant. Reginald was getting to be what Lorinda called "almost nice," so she just grinned at him and went right on reading. Duncan sighed. "You're lucky if you can get two words out of her since she started reading that old diary," he muttered to George.

George laughed. "Cheer up," he said. "I hear

there are only twenty-one volumes still to read."

"Twenty-one!"

"Yeah. Twenty-one. Her grandmother stopped writing them when she was thirty-four years old. Lorinda says she was too busy with all those kids she had and all. So she just stopped."

"Holy jumpin'!" groaned Duncan. "I bet we won't hardly even see her for the next twenty-one years."

James chuckled. "Don't give up hope so fast," he said. "She told me she was only going to read one a year — the year she's at when she reads it. So she won't be reading the last one till she's thirty-four."

"When she's thirty-four," said Duncan, looking a bit more cheerful, "she'll probably be too old to enjoy reading."

"C'mon, Lorinda," yelled Reginald. "Here comes the bus."

Lorinda followed the kids onto the bus like a sleep-walker, and then went right on reading.

Dear Diary: Today was the day after Norman's birthday. It was a Sunday, and I was scared to go outside, even to the corner store for a Polar Pie, because I was afraid he'd do it while I was away. I don't want to miss anything. Else how can I make my diary interesting? And complete.

At noon time we all sat down for Sunday dinner. It was chicken, as usual. For dessert, we had leftover birthday cake, and when everyone was finished and the cake was all gone and Mother and I were clearing away the dessert dishes, Norman said — very serious — "I have something I have to tell you all." To my amazement, Mother turned chalk-white and sat down. And I knew, right at that moment, that she'd been expecting this. Dad's head was down when Norman spoke, and he didn't raise it. He just looked up at him from his bent head.

"Yes?" he said, very quiet. And I knew he knew, too.

"I'm sorry," said Norman, and you could suddenly tell that he'd forgotten all the words he'd memorized.

"It's not that I want . . . I'm not sure how to . . . It's just that the Nazis do such terrible things. If I don't stop them, who will?"

Hilary looked sort of joyful and surprised and terrified at the same time.

"Just say it," said Dad, with his mouth hardly moving, like he was speaking through his teeth.

"I'm going to enlist tomorrow," said

Norman. He said it very softly, as though he was apologizing for something.

"Oh, _Norman_," sighed Mother, "does it have to be _now_?" She was rubbing her hands together almost like she was washing them or putting hand lotion on them. Rub, rub, rub. Like Hilary's thumbs. "Couldn't you wait a couple of months? The war might be over by then. You just finished exams. You must be tired. _Think_ about it, Norman."

"I _have_ been thinking about it, Mother," said Norman. "All year. And if everyone waits a couple of months before they enlist, the war sure isn't going to be over soon. And Dad?"

"Yes?" Dad raised his head a little, and looked as though he was trying to smile, but it wasn't working.

"I hope you know I don't want to go. Like, I don't think war is fun, or simple, or romantic, or any of those things. If I'm going, it's because I think I have to."

Dad took a long, long breath and let it out slowly. Then he said, "You're eighteen years old, Norman. You're free to do anything you feel you have to do. I can see that you're not whooping for joy yourself, so I hope you'll understand if we can't act very

104

thrilled about it." Dad's only forty-two years old, but he suddenly looked like an old man. And Mother. You should have seen Mother. She wasn't even looking at Norman. She was staring at the wall, and it was like she was seeing everything in the world that was sad and scary right there in front of her.

"Hey, wow!" Wouldn't you know that's what Eric would say?

He's so dumb it scares me. "You mean you're going to be a soldier or a sailor or an airman or something? Wait'll I tell Freddie!" Freddie's his best friend.

"Good idea," said Dad. "Go on over to Freddie's for a while."

And stay for ten years, I thought. You could see that Dad couldn't take much of that chipper-cheery stuff from Eric right then.

"Gee," said Eric, as he got up to go, "I sure hope the war keeps on long enough so I can go, too."

I wouldn't have thought that Mother could get any whiter, but she did. I was afraid she might faint or something. But instead, she started to cry — not in a boo-hoo way like a kid, but in a slow, soft, despairing sort of way. I thought Norman

would get to her first, but I was wrong. Old
frozen Hilary just shot across the room and
put her arms around Mother and held her
till she stopped.

Later on, long after everyone had gone
to bed, I could hear Dad down in the living-
room. Crying. In a strangled way, like Hil-
ary, but crying. Me, too. I cried a lot. What
a lot of crying in this house. But I guess
that's what war is all about. Not pipers'
bands or marching parades or people star-
ing bravely into the sunset. What war is
really about is a lot of crying.

Yours, Laura

"Lorinda! Are you all right?" That was Mrs.
MacDonald's voice, and Lorinda was in her home-
room at school. The diary was on her lap and she
was reading it between fractions and decimals.

"Fine, thanks," said Lorinda, shoving the diary
into her desk. "Just fine." But her voice broke a
little as she spoke. She pulled a handkerchief out
of her pocket and blew her nose hard.

That evening, Lorinda came into the kitchen
with her jacket on. It was nine-thirty and dark.

"Where do you think you're going at this hour?"
said Mrs. Dauphinee, her hands on her hips.

"To the store," said Lorinda. "I need some stuff

for school tomorrow, and the variety store's open till ten."

"What stuff?"

"Oh, you know. A new binder because my old one just fell apart. And a refill for my pen."

Ms. Dauphinee sighed. "You should be in your bed," she said. "And besides, I don't like you out on the roads at this hour. Anything could happen."

"Like *what*?" Lorinda could feel the old familiar fury rising in her. "Mom! I'll be *fine*. This is just a friendly little village. And I'm tall and strong. No one's going to kidnap me or hijack me or slit my throat. I have to have this stuff for school tomorrow. Or else Mrs. MacDonald will kill me."

Mrs. Dauphinee dug in her apron pocket and fished out five dollars. "Well, hurry, then," she sighed. "I'd go with you, only your dad's out, and I can't leave Jessie and James alone. Don't forget to walk on the left side of the road."

"Mom!" cried Lorinda. "Get off my back! I've been walking on the left side of the road since I was five years old. Don't be such a worry-wart. It's not like I'm going to *war*, or anything. I'm going to Coolen's Variety Store."

Lorinda was so mad that she almost forgot to walk on the left side. But she remembered in time, and within ten minutes she'd reached the store and made her purchases.

On the way back, she mused on her mother's

foolish fears, and felt more and more irritated. Staring at the ground, she paid no attention to the approaching car lights. But when the car swerved in her direction, she jumped onto the shoulder, ran across the ditch, and threw herself into some low bushes.

The car stopped, and she could tell as the door opened and the inside light came on, that these men — all three of them — were strangers to the Harbour. One of them was drinking from a bottle of beer, and the others were leering at her and laughing. The man who had opened the door had a fat unshaven face, and even by the dim light coming from the car, she could see the sweat glistening in the creases of his skin.

"Sorry about that!" he said, hiccupping loudly. "Just thought it would be fun to give you a little scare." He roared a sudden horrible laugh.

From across the ditch, Lorinda could smell the beer. It's like they've got a whole brewery in there, she thought.

"C'mon, sweetheart," said the man. He was already out of the car and reaching across the ditch. "Get in. We'll take you for a little ride."

For a moment Lorinda stood frozen, unable to move, with her heart beating so hard it felt as though it would pump a hole through her chest. Then she turned and ran like a wild thing through the woods, in the direction of the Dauphinee house. She could hear noises in the bushes behind her, and terror made her feet fly like wings.

It was a black and moonless night, and she was glad of it. She knew the footpath almost as well by night as by day — but surely the man behind her didn't. Once she heard a crash, a thud and the rustle of bushes, followed by loud cursing. Twice she tripped over a root herself, but she didn't fall. She just went on running, running, in the direction of home. Every turn and stone was familiar to her. She knew exactly when she was behind the MacDermid's gift shop, in front of Mr. Hyson's fence, beside her own barn, and then — at last — in view of the lights at her own back door.

Inside the back porch, Lorinda slammed the door, locked it, and leaned against it, eyes closed, panting. By the time her mother appeared from upstairs, she was breathing normally. She hoped Mrs. Dauphinee couldn't see her heart thumping in her neck.

"Hi, Mom," she said, very, very casually. Then she added, "I'm sorry."

"What?" Her mother looked puzzled. "What for?"

"Oh, I dunno," said Lorinda. "I guess for snapping at you. And for not realizing."

"Not realizing what?"

"That wars aren't the only things in the world that are scary."

Then Lorinda kissed her mother on the cheek and climbed the stairs to bed.

"Sometimes," said Mrs. Dauphinee as she joined her husband in the living-room, "I think that maybe Helen MacDermid is right. Lorinda *is* an odd sort of child."

11

Lorinda had gone to bed late, but she awoke
early. Once she was fully awake, she lay in
bed and thought about Norman going to war. She
could hear the wind outside the window, and the
cold March sea sloshing around the piles under
the stages. What would it be like on those warships in the middle of winter — at night, cold and
dark and blacked out; by day, grey and frozen and
full of fear? She knew a lot more about fear now
than she had known yesterday morning. She knew
how it clutched your whole body and filled your
throat till you could almost taste it.

Lorinda realized there weren't many pages left
in the diary for age thirteen, and she wondered
if she should save it to make it last, or . . . But
no. She couldn't. Jessie was still fast asleep, and
she slept, as Mr. Dauphinee said, like a rock —
heavier by far than a log. So Lorinda turned on
her light and opened the diary.

Dear Diary: Today Norman enlisted. It was awful. I don't think I can talk about it, even to you. I can't stand to see Mother and Dad suffer like this. I'm not sure I'll ever be brave enough to be a parent, now. When you get a new baby, you must just think, it's a BABY. You know — you buy bootees and little sweaters and hug it a lot. You feed it and comfort it, and it must be a really lovely feeling. But what you can't be thinking is, when this baby grows up and gets big, he's going to go off and be in a war. How could you stand even looking at him if you knew that? If I had a little baby boy and he grew up and there was a war on, I think I'd tie him up and lock him in a room somewhere until the fighting was all over.

No. I don't think I want to write any more today.

Sincerely, lower than a snake's belly,
Laura

Well, thought Lorinda, that certainly didn't tell me very much. She turned the page.

Dear Diary: I'm sorry I've been neglecting you. It's summer now, and we're out of school, and Norman is away somewhere (we're not allowed to know where) learning how to be a sailor. Eric really misses him, and he's not quite as wild and silly any more. But almost.

Nothing's the way it used to be. Mother and Dad try to act happy, but it doesn't fool me. When the phone rings, they jump about a mile off their chairs, and when a letter comes from Norman, they read it so hard that even an earthquake wouldn't disturb them. The roof could fall right in, and they'd just go on reading.

Things were a little bit better this past week because Geoffrey's ship was in port, and he came to see us three times. Three visits. Three baths. He told Hilary that when he was in England last month he went to see her house. Her mother was away, but he saw the flowers in the garden and a little bird house, and even remembered what the curtains looked like in the windows. She just sat and listened to him talk, with her eyes hungry, and her body so still that you'd have thought she was paralyzed.

Eileen plays with Judith all the time, even though they fight a lot. I've got Hilary, and she'd be perfect if she'd just soften up

113

*a little. Unbend. She's almost never unbent
except when Geoffery's around to bewitch
her. You can't have a best friend who never
tells you her secrets or troubles.*

Fed up, Laura

Lorinda wasn't used to these short entries, but
she read on.

*Dear Diary: Today I asked Hilary about
her parents. She said, "I used to be angry
at my mother all the time, but now I think
maybe she was almost perfect."*

I asked her why she got mad.

*She shrugged her shoulders and said,
"Oh, you know — the usual things. It both-
ered me that she reminded me about everything — about wearing my jumper if it was
cold, or taking my brollie if it was raining,
or eating vegetables I didn't like. And she
didn't want me to do dangerous things."*

"Such as?"

*"Such as swimming way out to sea or
doing back dives."*

"Back dives? Can you do back dives?"

*"Yes. Or I used to be able to. But she was
so sure I'd snap my spine in two and be-
come a quadriplegic that after a time I became too frightened to try them any more."*

114

I told her that I understood exactly how she felt. But she said no I didn't, because she didn't feel like that any more. She said, "It was certainly irritating, but I realize now that she just did things like that because she loved me."

Well, I'm not going to nag my kids into a state of frazzlement. I'm going to let them grow up strong and brave and independent, and I won't pay any attention to whether it's cold or rainy or whether they eat vegetables. Or of course whether they keep their rooms tidy. I plan to be a perfect mother.

Confidently, Laura

Well, thought Lorinda, with a grim smile, I hope you at least nag them about keeping off the highway after dark. Then she continued to read.

Dear Diary: This was an eventful day. Today I met Ian over by St. Thomas Aquinas School where everybody plays softball. We didn't play softball, though. We talked. He said he thought the parents of the Guest Children were the bravest and most noble people in the world. I asked him why. He said, "They love their children and want to keep them nearby. But they've sent them far across the ocean so they'll be safe."

I said I couldn't see why that was so terribly brave, and he said wouldn't I mind if my parents sent Eric away to a safe place? And I said I wouldn't even care if they sent him away to an <u>unsafe</u> place. Then he got kind of mad and said didn't I understand about the way parents loved their children, and I thought about Norman and said yes, I did.

Then I said, "But they'll come home safe after the war. Maybe Norman won't." Ian was sitting on the fence practising "Around the World" with his yo-yo, and making it sleep, so he didn't answer for a minute. But then he said, "When Norman comes back, he'll be a lot like he is now, because he's eighteen already. He'll be somewhat different perhaps, but not radically. Unless his nerves deteriorate." Do you see what I mean about the way these English kids talk?

Then he said something I never even thought of. He said, "When our parents get us back, we're all going to be totally different. We'll have Canadian accents and we'll be asking why there isn't any peanut butter, and we'll be mad because things are more formal over there, and not so free and easy. And we'll bore them silly with stories about canoe trips and central heating, and we'll laugh when they call overshoes galoshes and running shoes, pumps. And we'll look different. We'll be older and bigger, and we'll be wearing clothes that they wouldn't be caught dead in. And we'll feel like foreigners . . ." he paused, ". . . in our own land."

I said I thought that was awful, and would it really be that bad? He said yes, it <u>would</u> be that bad. "And besides," he went on, "when the Guest Children go home, some of them won't stay."

"Where will they go?"

"Back. Back here. Where they have discovered they want to be."

It wrecked my day just to think of anything that sad — although it did cross my mind that it would suit me very well if Ian decided to come back here because it was where he "discovered he wanted to be."

Then he said, "And what's more, our parents aren't stupid. They knew all those things. And yet they did it. They sent us away to keep us alive. Not for them. For us."

I said, "You mean there's almost no way
they can really cash in on it?"
"Exactly!" he said.
No siree. I don't think I'm up to being a
parent at all.

                              Sincerely, Laura

When Lorinda came to the end of the entry,
she looked out the window without moving for a
long time. It was still too dark to see anything,
but even if it had been broad, bright daylight, she
still wouldn't have noticed what was out there.
She was thinking about Jessie, and that's all she
could see, inside her head. She was trying to imagine what it would be like to send Jessie away —
Jessie — way across the sea to another country.
Then she thought about Jessie coming back, five
years later, ten and one half years old — as old
as James — and completely different. Maybe the
curl would have all grown out of her hair; perhaps
she'd be long and spindly instead of small and firm
and nice to hold on your lap; she might even be
wearing glasses like James. In her head, Lorinda
could see this unfamiliar person coming in the
front door of their house (because she'd forgotten
that everyone used the back door) and saying, in
a strange new voice, "I'm back. I'm home. But I
wish I wasn't. Why does this house have to look

                          118

so peculiar? And why doesn't someone fix the porch? I hope you're not expecting me to stay here."

Lorinda turned over and buried her face in the pillow. Then she crept out of bed and crossed the room to Jessie's bed. There she was — five and a half years old, and still there. Lorinda sighed. This diary, she thought, is exhausting me. But she picked it up again, and read on.

Dear Diary: Yesterday we got word that Geoffrey had been killed. His ship was torpedoed. Hilary went up to her room, and I heard her making her choking noises. Now he'll never go and see her house again. He was like her last link to home. And now he'll never come here any more and yell "Hi!" and rush upstairs to run his bath. And I know what we're all thinking. We can't help it. We're thinking, it could be Norman. Because Norman's out there on a ship, too. I don't want to write any more tonight.

Sorrowfully, Laura

Lorinda closed her eyes and took a long, deep breath. When she opened her eyes, she could see the sky filling up with daylight, and the harbour calm again after the night's wind. She closed the diary carefully and put it under her pillow.

"How come you're not reading?" said a small voice from across the room. It was Jessie.

"Because," said Lorinda, "although it's only seven o'clock in the morning, I've had all I can take for one day."

12

That day, Lorinda did cheerful things. She joked with Duncan on the school bus, teased Reginald Corkum about his new rubber boots, and admired the Bay from the window. At school, she finished her project on Mexico, and ate half of James's lunch and all of her own.

It was still cold, so after school she and George and Duncan went skating on Black Lake. Then, when she'd finished the supper dishes, she watched TV and had a game of Crib with her father. But at bedtime, she was ready for more. More diary, that is. She crawled into bed and started to read.

Dear Diary: Yesterday, in the middle of the night, there were terrible sounds. Guns and bombs and shooting — real war sounds. I sat up in bed and listened, hold-

ing the covers around me like I was frozen, although it was hot in the house. It's hard to believe, but Mother and Dad and Eric slept through it. It was exactly like the Nazis and Hitler were right down in the harbour, ready to destroy Halifax. I was going to go in and wake Mother and Dad, but just then Hilary came in. She was holding her blue kimono around her like she was cold, too, and inside her kimono you could see Agatha, all squashed against her chest. She said, "I thought you might be startled, so I came in to keep you company."

There she was, scruffed-up pigtails from sleeping on them, those round glasses on her nose, eyes bugging right out. And I thought, boy, is she ever brave. Then her face sort of collapsed like it was made of too-soft plasticine, and she started to cry. Her arms dropped down to her sides and Agatha fell to the floor. Hilary didn't even bother to blow her nose or cover her screwed-up mouth. She cried out loud in a way that was a lot like screaming.

Mother and Dad may have slept through the war sounds, but they didn't sleep through Hilary. They came running in with Eric, while she was still heaving and sobbing.

"I can't stand it!" she yelled. "I can't stand being frightened and sad any more!" She kept repeating, over and over again, "I can't stand it! I can't stand it!" Then she put her hands over her ears and cried out, "Make it stop!"

Then we were all hugging her. I mean really all of us. Eric was hugging her legs because it was the only part he could get at. Mother was murmuring, "There! There!" and smoothing the back of her head. I was hugging from the back, and Dad, having long arms, had them around all of us.

When Hilary finally stopped crying, we all sat down on the bed, and she looked at us through her crooked (from being hugged) glasses, and said, "You're all crying. Not just me." And we all laughed in a stuttery kind of way, and then she gave a great big long sigh and said,

"Oh! That felt so good! I think I'll have a big howl like that once a week for the rest of my life!"

The next day we heard that the navy had to sink one of our own big cargo ships —

right in the harbour — because it was full
of ammunition (that's bullets and bombs
and grenades and stuff like that) and it was
on fire. They were afraid there might be
another explosion like in the First World
War. If Hilary had known that, she'd prob-
ably have collapsed in a heap, just like the
ship.

Sincerely amazed, Laura

Aha, thought Lorinda. *Thawed.* And about
time, too. Then she continued to read.

Dear Diary: I haven't written hardly at all
because we've been having too much fun.
We went to Cow Bay for two weeks, and
swam every day and went skinny-dipping
on the beach at night.

Hilary and I are best friends now. Some-
times we have little fights, but that's fine.
I didn't know she could fight before. Or cry
or complain or whoop for joy. Now she's
all loosened up and can do all those things.
She's really funny and fun.

And pretty, too. We both cut our hair last
week, and do we ever look different. I was
jealous at first, because Hilary looked a lot
better than I did. I was so used to her look-

*ing like a little old owl that it was a shock
to see what short hair did to her face. She's
got naturally curly hair and it's thick, too.
She also has a small nose and a big wide
grin. I felt like an ugly duckling.*

*My hair is straight and hasn't any
bounce in it. But Mother said we both
looked terrific, and that she was proud to
walk down the street with two such beautiful young women. So then we laughed,
and it was all right.*

*I'm only thirteen, but I heard a grown-
up say once that I had good bones. That
means that by the time I'm eighteen I'll be
ravishingly beautiful. Maybe by sixteen.*

*Hilary seems really happy now, and so
am I. Sometimes for a whole day at a time,
I forget all about there being a war. But
often you can't forget. At night we hear
airplanes and watch the searchlights moving back and forth, back and forth, trying
to trap the planes in their light. And when
they do, it's very beautiful until you realize
that if someone shot at them right then,
they probably wouldn't miss.*

Sincerely, Laura

Lorinda jumped out of bed and padded down

the hall in her bare feet. When she reached the bathroom, she turned on the light above the sink and looked at herself in the mirror. Pale face; big brown eyes; long straggly black hair, straight as a stick. She gathered up her long hair and arranged it so that it looked short. Not great, she thought, but not one hundred percent terrible, either.

Mrs. Dauphinee poked her head around the corner of the door and grinned. "Mrs. MacDermid was wrong," she said. "I like it better long. Besides . . ."

"Besides what?" Lorinda had let her hair drop down again.

"Besides," repeated Mrs. Dauphinee, "people with good bones are the only ones who really look nice in long hair."

Lorinda kissed her mother on the cheek as she turned out the light. "Thanks, Mom," she said. Then she returned to her room and went on reading.

Dear Diary: Something terrible has happened. Not as bad as Norman getting killed, but almost. Hilary's father is missing. Missing. His plane didn't come back from a bombing mission, and no one knows where he is or how he is. Or even if he is.

I don't know how Hilary stands it, but now that she talks a lot, she lets us know how she feels, and that gets rid of some of her fear and sadness. That's what Mother says, anyway. She says that it will be hard for her but that she'll be able to bear it. Me, I think missing must be almost worse than dead. If you don't <u>know</u>, you keep thinking of a lot of terrible things. Like: Where is he? Is he wounded? Is there anyone to look after him? What if the Nazis find him and shoot him? Or put him in a concentration camp? Is he in terrible pain?

Dad says that it is good to be able to hope, but my imagination is too grisly for me to be very good at hoping. Ian came over and talked to Hilary, and she felt a lot better after that. He told her that the Underground keep a watch out for pilots who parachute over their territory. He said her father could easily be sitting in a nice French cottage right now, eating onion soup and sipping wine.

Sometimes it seems to me that Ian is about thirty years old. I'm surprised that he can have a cousin like Judith who seems so lah-dee-dah and self-centred. But maybe I'm just mad at her because Eileen likes

*her better than me. Maybe she's okay. She
tries to be friendly to me sometimes, but
I'm just not the fish that's going to take her
hook.*

Worried, Laura

Wow! thought Lorinda. And I thought for a few
minutes that all I had to worry about was whether
or not to cut my hair! She read on.

*Dear Diary: Tomorrow is school again. It's
hard to believe it's been almost a year since
the Guest Children came over. They seemed
so strange, and I guess we were all scared
of each other. Now we're all just one big
soup. The noodles are still noodles, and the
split peas are still peas, but together they
make the soup more delicious.*

*I don't know which of us are the noodles
and which are the peas, but I do know that
our school won't be half as nice when those
kids go back home.*

Yours, Laura

Lorinda yawned and the diary fell out of her
hands onto the floor. She didn't even hear it fall.
While she slept, she dreamt that she was a member of the Underground and that she was saving
Hilary's father from a band of Nazi soldiers. There

was a lot of shooting, and the explosions were terrible.

When she woke up, she found that the explosions were the waves pounding on Elbow Beach, and that the rat-tat-tat of bullets was really hail on the roof of the old porch. And it was morning.

13

Several days passed before Lorinda had time to read any more of the diary. There was a late deep snowstorm in the last week of March, and the kids spent every spare hour they could find coasting, tobogganing, snowshoeing. Each day, Duncan would arrive at the door, close his eyes tight, and recite, "Lorinda, how'd you like to go tobogganing today?" — or snowshoeing or coasting or whatever. Every time, she'd recite right back, "Why Duncan, I'd love to."

One of the things they enjoyed most was sliding down Mr. Hyson's Hill on old heavy salt bags. They were forever hanging around the wharves begging for bags from the fishermen. As Duncan said, "It's the next best thing to going down on the seat of your pants." Seeing as no one's parents wanted their kids to slide the seats right out of their pants, it was plastic salt bags or nothing.

But on Sunday, there was a thaw, and the outside world wasn't good for anything. There was no ice for skating, and the snow was just a blanket of grey slush. "A good day for reading," said Lorinda to James at breakfast. James had started to read the diary himself (when Lorinda was busy elsewhere) and he could hardly wait for her to finish the book so he could have it all to himself. At first Lorinda hadn't known if she should show the diary to anyone else. So she'd asked her mother. After all, Laura was her mother. Who else could she ask?

Mrs. Dauphinee had thought for a few minutes, and then she had said, "I don't know, Lorinda. It's a really tough question. And I think it's one you have to answer yourself. After all, the only person she said shouldn't read them was Dad, to protect him from old boyfriends and old secrets. She knew how worried and depressed he gets over little things. But if you read one of those diaries and you know it won't hurt the reader — like James, for instance — and if you want to share it, then go ahead. They're yours now. She gave them to you. You decide."

So now James and Lorinda could talk about Grandma and her family as though they were old mutual friends. "I'm not gonna save reading those other ones till I'm the same age as Grandma," announced James. "If it's okay with you, I think I'll go right straight through to age thirty-four."

"Well," said Lorinda, "it's *not* okay with me. It's very nice of me to let you read them at all. But I can't put up with you learning all her secrets before I do. Besides, there might be girl stuff in them that would be bad for you to read."

"Like what?" asked James.

"Like . . . oh, *you know*."

"I suppose so. But I'd like to read about her having babies and stuff like that."

"If that's *all* she talks about, fine. But it's me that's gonna find out first. And don't worry about me waiting till I'm thirty-four to read about Grandma at thirty-four. I know now I could never wait that long. Do you think I can wait till I'm fourteen to find out if Norman's going to be okay? Or if they find Hilary's father? No siree!"

Up in her room, Lorinda took out the diary. There weren't many pages left.

Dear Diary: Four weeks to my birthday, and then I'll be fourteen. I got my period last week. Now I'm a full-fledged woman. And do you know something else? So did Hilary. Did you ever hear of anything so weird? I'm starting to get breasts, but they're so small that Mother calls them mosquito bites. Hilary is still as flat as a board. I'm ashamed to admit it, but I'm glad I'm ahead of her in something. She's

132

*so smart in school that sometimes I feel
like a colonial dummy. But she says she
hates being with all those old girls, some
of them fifteen or even sixteen, crowding
around the washroom mirror all the time
at recess, putting on their yucky lipsticks.
Then they wipe most of it off and hope that
Miss Leroy won't notice it's there at all. I
don't know why they bother. Hilary likes
some of the kids in grade 10, but she doesn't
play with them. I guess nobody plays when
they're that old anyway.*

*Hilary says she likes best to play with
me because I make her feel comfortable and
safe. Maybe that's not as good as being
smart and beautiful, but it's something.*

Sincerely,
The Aging Laura

Lorinda ran her hand down the front of her
sweater. Like Hilary, she thought. Flat as a
board.

*Dear Diary: I haven't been writing to you
because I've been busy writing a story for
the school magazine. I love writing stories
and poems. I can hardly wait to grow up
so I can get to be an author. I intend to be
rich and famous. I'll walk into a bookstore,*

and all my books will be lined up on the display table. And some lady in a mink coat will rush over and say (humbly), "Would it be too much trouble for you to give me your autograph?" I'll turn very slowly, very casually, and say, "Why no. I'd be happy to. I just happen to have a few moments to spare."

Maybe I'll stop writing diaries and start writing novels.

Yours, The Author, Laura

"I sure hope not," muttered Lorinda, turning the page.

Dear Diary: Sometimes Hilary gets really down in the dumps about her father. One day she said, "I can't bear it if he's in a concentration camp eating old potato skins and having no one to set his broken leg."

I said, "How do you know they eat potato skins? And what broken leg?"

She said she just figured in concentration camps they probably ate watery soup and potato skins. And that she just dreamed up the broken leg. Bet I'd be doing things like that, too. Thinking the worst.

Yours, Laura

Dear Diary: I got ten out of ten in math today. Hilary's been teaching me. Eileen only got six. I was glad.

In triumph, Laura

I'm surprised, thought Lorinda, that she can even think of math marks when Hilary's father may be hunched over somewhere, eating watery soup and potato skins. But she continued to read.

Dear Diary: One night I sat straight up in bed and thought, how could we ever get out of this city if something awful ever happened to it? Halifax is a peninsula. It's sort of like a balloon, and it joins the rest of the province by the neck of the balloon. Not that small, but not very big, either. That night I was listening to the terrible wail of the practise air raid sirens, and I thought, if the city ever starts to burn up or anything — all those hundreds and hundreds of wooden houses — the only way to get out is through that little neck. That was a scary thought. I didn't mention this to Hilary. She's got enough to worry about already.

Yours, filled with fears, awash with worry,

Laura

Dear Diary: You'll never guess. Something amazing. Hilary got a phone call from her mother in England. It must have cost a million pounds. Pounds are what they have in England instead of dollars. I couldn't believe her mother's accent. <u>So strong</u>. And I realized Hilary has lost a lot of hers. And do you know what her mother said? She said, "Hilary! You have a Canadian accent!" That's pretty funny, eh? We think she's losing her English accent. They think she's gaining a Canadian accent. I wonder what it sounds like in their ears.

Anyway, Hilary's mother spent all that money to call because her father isn't missing any more! Ian was right. He was rescued by the Underground, and he's staying in whatever country it is (they couldn't tell her which) to help the Underground army do whatever it is they do. If he can get out of the country and home, he will. But it's tricky. After all, England's an island. The Underground people got word over to England somehow or other. Mrs. Sutcliffe couldn't talk long. Too expensive.

Hilary is walking on air. She says her father is still in great danger, but not like when you're up in a plane with people shooting at you all the time. And the main thing is — he's not missing any more.

Dad looked as relieved as if it had been his own brother. Mother wasn't around for the call. She was out serving coffee and cocoa in one of the army canteens downtown where she's always working. But she lit up like a Christmas tree when she came home and we told her.

Mother's really tired from her work in the canteens and from forever feeding servicemen and women at home. She doesn't complain, but I can see it in her face. Sometimes she looks sort of droopy, and not so spick-and-span and perfect any more. The droopiness probably comes from worrying about Norman. Anyway, when she heard about Hilary's father, all the droop disappeared, and she went to Hilary and hugged her a long, long time.

Tomorrow's my birthday.

Yours, relieved, Laura

Sept. 3. My birthday!

Dear Diary: I'm tired after a long day, but I have to write at least something before I go to bed. My birthday was beautiful. The only bad part was Norman not being here.

I'm fourteen now. A real teenager. Thirteen is really only half a teenager. Mother and Dad gave me a wrist-watch. I killed my old one when I dove into the North West Arm wearing it. Eric gave me a big blank book (red) with lines in it. I didn't know he could be that smart, but Mother says it was his own idea. He looked really happy that I was pleased with it, and I thought, Eric, I'm three-quarters on the way to liking you.

Hilary got me a little chain with a pearl on it. She has a paper route, and I bet she must have spent about three weeks' money on it. Eileen came over, looking kind of embarrassed, and gave me some bath salts. Judith tagged along too, of course, and she brought a card.

I wish I could make myself like Judith, because try as I will, I can't think of one single thing she does that's bad. I even think that maybe she wants me to like her. I can feel it in the air. I guess I'm just sad because she stole Eileen. But you can't even blame her for that, what with them living in the same house and all. Life is just so complicated, and sometimes even if you think hard, you can't work things out.

Ian came over and gave me a wonderful,

perfect, round grey rock that he picked up on a beach in St. Margaret's Bay. It has dark red lines weaving through it, almost like veins, and it's very, very beautiful. When you put it in water, the colours change. I'll keep it forever and ever.

Well, dear Diary, that's all for this year. Tomorrow I start a new book, and even though I have two others, I think I'll use Eric's. I feel kind of friendly to Eric tonight.

Goodnight. It's been nice being with you this past year.

Sincerely, Old, but happy, Laura

Lorinda closed the diary, and held it for a moment between the palms of both hands. She looked out the window, but she wasn't seeing the gulls or the lighthouse or Pony Island. She was seeing a whole mental movie: the school with so many English Guest Children; Norman delivering his bad news; Hilary's father in his bomber; the scene after Hilary's phone call from home; the birthday party; Eric presenting the red book. She felt as though she had been in a whole other world.

"Thank you, Grandma," she said, right out loud. "Thank you, Laura, for bringing yourself to me."

"What?" asked Jessie, poking her curly head in the doorway as she passed by.

"Oh, nothing," said Lorinda. "Just talking to someone you've never met."

In the afternoon, Lorinda took the diary into James's room. "Here," she said. "Now you can finish it. And James?"

"Yeah?"

"I'm gonna ask Mom about Norman. He's still okay in the diary, but I can't wait for maybe four years of his life to find out. I just don't happen to be that patient."

"Well, I am," said James. "So when you find out, don't tell me."

"Okay," agreed Lorinda. "And James . . ."

But he didn't answer. He was already a long way away — in Halifax. Many, many years ago.

14

That afternoon, rain continued to pour onto the sodden snow. Patches of brown grass started to appear here and there, particularly on Mr. Hyson's Hill. The rain was coming down in such torrents that Pony Island was just a ghostly form, and you couldn't see the buoys at all. You could just hear the dim *mmmmmmuh* of the Groaner Buoy beyond the clatter of the rain and the rattling of the storm windows in the gusts of wind. A good day, thought Lorinda, to bring myself up to date on history. If she could just find a moment when her mother was free. But that turned out to be far from easy.

First, Lorinda found her in the kitchen, making cookies.

"Mom," she said, "gotta second? I want to ask you some questions."

"Not right this minute," said Mrs. Dauphinee, her head bent low over a recipe book. "I've never made these before, and if I talk while I'm doing it, I'm apt to put salt in them instead of sugar. Or forget the nuts. Come around later."

When Lorinda came back half an hour later, the last cookies were coming out of the oven. "How 'bout I wash your baking dishes," said Lorinda, helping herself to a cookie, "and we can talk?"

"Fine," agreed her mother.

But Lorinda barely had the water in the pan before Jessie turned up, chatter-chatter-chattering about her doll, her puzzle, the rain, the cookies, the scab on her knee.

With the dishes done and Jessie gone, Lorinda thought the moment had come. But no. Just as she was about to corner her mother, in came James, searching for the peanut butter. "It's not where it should be," he said. "Where the heck is it?" They all went to look, but it was only when they passed the living room that they found it.

There sat Jessie, at her little play table, with toy dishes laid out in front of each of four dolls. There were four crackers at each place, and every cracker was piled high with peanut butter.

"By the time we eat all those," said Lorinda, "the crackers'll be like moosh."

Then it was time to get another meal. They were having supper early because Mr. Dauphinee hadn't gone out lobstering that day. "No point in encouraging that bronchitis to start up again," said Mrs. Dauphinee. "The lobsters'll still be there tomorrow."

Then, believe it or not, Mr. and Mrs. Himmelman came over for coffee, bringing George and Glynis. Everyone sat around and talked, and the kids played a game of Monopoly. After they left, Mr. Dauphinee wanted his wife to watch his favourite TV program with him. As she untied her apron and went off to join him, Mrs. Dauphinee gave Lorinda a little pat and said, "We're not having much luck, are we, Lorinda? But unless there's a full-fledged king-sized crisis, I promise you I won't go to bed before we have our talk."

So Lorinda went and got ready for bed herself while her parents watched TV. Jessie was fast asleep, and James was in his room reading the diary. He'd only left it long enough to eat supper and play Monopoly.

Lorinda crawled into bed and hauled out a mystery she'd been reading before she went to Vancouver. Pretty tame stuff, she thought, after that diary.

Finally, at ten o'clock, Mrs. Dauphinee tiptoed into Lorinda's bedroom. "Let's go down to the kitchen," she whispered. "The stove's still on, so it's nice and warm. And we can make some hot chocolate."

At last, with Lorinda sitting up at the table and her mother sipping her hot chocolate in the big wooden rocker, they were ready.

"Mom," said Lorinda, "I've just finished Grandma's first big diary. I'm gonna go back and read the earlier ones later, but I wanted to know her at age thirteen, right this minute. But now my head is nearly crazy with questions, and I know I can't wait to find out the answers till I read all the later diaries. *I just have to know.* Like . . ."

"Like what?" prompted her mother.

"Like — I hate to ask, because I'm scared of the answer — did Norman come back home from the war safe? Did anything awful happen to him?"

"Norman? Oh — *Uncle* Norman. My Uncle Norman. He was always just a name to me."

"Mom! Answer me! Did he get back from the war okay?"

"Yes. Yes, he did. He had some little wound that brought him home before the war was over. And I remember now that Mother once said that a wound never was so welcome, never looked so good. She said that when her own father heard Norman was wounded — but not badly — he went around looking like he'd seen a vision. He had a head wound, I think, that made him a little bit deaf. You can't keep someone in the navy who's a little bit deaf."

Lorinda closed her eyes. "Oh, Mom!" she

breathed. "What a relief! But . . ."

"Yes?"

"How come you never knew him? After all, he was your uncle."

"Because when he was about twenty-four, he went back to England. He'd been stationed there during the war, and he loved it. He never came back. Not to live. He did come for a few visits — but much later, when I wasn't living at home. My own dad was in the navy, and that meant he and Mother were always getting shunted around, all over the country, and sometimes even overseas. Heaven knows where they were living when Uncle Norman made his visits."

"You poor thing!" muttered Lorinda.

"Who?" Mrs. Dauphinee looked startled. "Me? Why?"

"Because you never met Norman." Lorinda sighed.

Mrs. Dauphinee laughed. "You're really deep into those diaries, aren't you! Anything else you want to know?"

"Well . . ." Lorinda hesitated. "I don't want to know too much, in case it spoils the next ones I read. The suspense and all. But there's one other thing I don't think I can wait to hear."

"What's that? I mightn't even know."

There was a pause while they listened to the rain clattering on the porch roof.

"Mom. What's Grandpa's first name?"

"Andrew."

"What a drag!" Lorinda sighed again. "But I guess I knew it couldn't be, anyway. Not unless he changed his last name. But I thought maybe he might do that, being as it sounds so crazy."

Mrs. Dauphinee grinned. "What on earth are you talking about?"

"Ian. I'm talking about Ian. I just kind of hoped that he'd married Grandma. He was such a great person. And I'm almost sure that Grandma loved him."

"How old did you say they were?"

"Grandma was thirteen. And Ian was fourteen. But *very mature* and very wise and kind."

"Well," said her mother, "a whole lot can happen between ages thirteen and fourteen and marrying-time. What did you say his name was?"

"Ian."

"Ian . . . Ian what?"

"Ian Ramsay-Davis. That's why I thought maybe he might have changed his name. And because of Grandpa's name being Davison."

"Ramsay-Davis. Yes, that rings a bell somewhere." Mrs. Dauphinee suddenly sat up straight in her rocking chair. "Brother Dominique!" she cried.

"Who? What?"

"Ian Ramsay-Davis. That's who he became —

146

Brother Dominique. Mother and Dad used to get letters from him. I never knew why, and I guess I was too busy with my own life and my own concerns to be very interested."

"You mean he was a priest, or something?"

"He was a monk. He worked with a leper colony in Africa."

"Lepers! You don't mean real *lepers*! Like in the *Bible*?"

"Yes. I do mean real lepers. You don't have to be in the Bible to have leprosy." Mrs. Dauphinee laughed. Then she stopped. "Leprosy isn't funny," she said, and then laughed again. "But *you* are!"

"But, Mom." Lorinda's eyes were large. "Wouldn't he get leprosy? Isn't it catching?"

"Gosh, Lorinda," said her mother. "You'd think to hear you that you really knew him!"

"I do!" cried Lorinda. "Quick! Tell me! Did he die?"

Mrs. Dauphinee paused. "Do you really want to know? You'll probably know everything anyway, before you get to the last diary."

Lorinda sighed. "I don't think I even need to ask," she said.

"Yes," said Mrs. Dauphinee. "He died. But not so very long ago. I remember Mother mentioning it. When he was about fifty-six, I think. But that's all I know. I wasn't paying enough attention to ask for more details. I never met him — unlike you."

Lorinda put her elbows on the table and her head in her hands.

Mrs. Dauphinee got out of her rocking chair and came over to sit down at the table beside Lorinda. She put her arm around her shoulders.

"Try not to be too sad," she said. "I'm sure he had an amazing and very satisfying life. And it can't be easy to find people willing to go and look after lepers. And I know that Grandma loved Grandpa very much."

"Oh, Mom!" groaned Lorinda. "Life is just so confusing. Nothing seems to be simple." She paused while the rain continued to beat against the windows. "I guess I never could have met him anyway. And I wouldn't have found out about it in the diaries, because he would have been thirty-five when Grandma stopped writing them. He'd be sixty-three now, and probably a leper, and in Africa." She suddenly had a thought. "Mom!" she almost shouted. "Is Norman still alive? Is he? *Is he?*"

"Well, yes," said her Mother, getting up and fishing around in a little drawer beside the sink. "I'm pretty sure he is. Sometimes he sends us a Christmas card. And maybe you'd like to write to him. I'm looking for my address book. I'm sure I've got Uncle Norman and Aunt Hilary's address in there somewhere. Yes. Here it is."

"Aunt *Hilary!*" This time Lorinda really did yell. "Mom! You don't mean to tell me that he married *Hilary!*"

Mrs. Dauphinee chuckled. "Lorinda, you'd better pipe down, or everyone in Blue Harbour is going to be awake. Well," she went on, "he certainly married some kind of Hilary. I hope it's the same one, because you seem awfully pleased." Mrs. Dauphinee stopped talking and thought hard for a moment. "Seems to me she came over to Canada for a few years from England when the war was on. When she was just a kid. Yes. Stayed with Mother's family. Would that be the same Hilary?"

"Mom!" Lorinda turned and hugged her mother until Mrs. Dauphinee's ribs ached. "You can't believe what a present you just gave me!" Then she sat up again. "Listen, Mom," she went on. "I've got just one more question. Just a little one. Not really important. But when you were growing up and living in your own house, did you ever see a rock around anywhere?"

"A *what?*"

"A rock. It would be round and grey and perfect. There would be little red lines running through it, and it would be very beautiful."

"Oh!" said her mother, her voice full of wonder. "*That* rock. Yes. That rock was around all through my childhood and for as long as I can remember. Every time we moved, out it came, and it always sat in a special place. Like on the mantelpiece or on the round mahogany table that Mother's own mother gave her for a wedding present. We always — Joan and I and the boys — teased her about the rock, and asked her to tell us why she liked it so much. But she never told us. She just said it was a gift from a dear friend. Lorinda, why was it special? Maybe you can tell me. Joan and I might get a good laugh out of it."

"No, Mom," said Lorinda, giving her mother's hand a little squeeze. "I don't think I want you and Aunt Joan having a good laugh out of it. I think you'd better just keep it as one of your unsolved mysteries. But I can tell you one thing about it."

"Yes?"

"It means that she kept a promise she made on her fourteenth birthday." Lorinda was quiet for a few moments. Then she looked at her mother. "Lookit," she said. "I'm so mixed up that I hardly know where I'm at. Since reading the diary, I feel like I've got Grandma back. And I feel like I've just lost Ian, who was dead when I was only seven years old. And now you've given me back Norman and Hilary. So I've got all these people walking in and out of my head."

Mrs. Dauphinee got up out of her chair and went over to the sink to put the cocoa pot to soak.

"Maybe," she said, "you'll understand it better after you've slept on it. You could use a little sleep, you know. And so could I. It's eleven-thirty, and both of us have to be up early. Take your friends and your thoughts to bed with you. Perhaps by morning everything'll look simpler." She put her hand on Lorinda's cheek and kissed the tip of her nose.

So that's what Lorinda did. She went upstairs and slipped under the heavy quilt, suddenly very tired. She missed having the diary to read at bedtime, and her hands felt empty. If there's one thing I learned from that diary, she said to herself, it's that no matter when or where you live, thirteen never really changes all that much. And that's a comforting sort of thing to find out.

"Tomorrow," she mumbled out loud as she drifted closer to sleep, "maybe I'll begin reading a new one." Her eyes flickered open again. "Or then again, I might play chess with Duncan. He got a new set for his birthday."

Then Lorinda grinned. "But I do know one thing I'm going to do for sure tomorrow," she said to the ceiling. "I'm going to buy myself one of those big black hardcover blank books. They've got them at Coolen's Variety Store. My own diary is too little to hold all the things I've started thinking about. And a lot of pretty interesting things are happening in my life. It's time I wrote them all down for my grandchildren."

Then Lorinda closed her eyes. In less than three seconds, she was asleep.

About the Author

BUDGE WILSON grew up in the Halifax of Lorinda's grandmother — in fact, she was thirteen years old when the English Guest Children sailed into Halifax Harbour. Her vivid memories of that time make this new tale of the Dauphinee family one of her best.

This award-winning author's works include *The Best / Worst Christmas Present Ever*, *A House Far from Home*, and *Mystery Lights at Blue Harbour* — all about the Blue Harbour Dauphinees. Her most recent book is the critically acclaimed *Breakdown*.

Ms. Wilson has recently returned to Nova Scotia where she plans to continue her writing.

APPLE® PAPERBACKS

Pick an Apple and Polish Off Some Great Reading!

BEST-SELLING APPLE TITLES

❑ MT43944-8	**Afternoon of the Elves** Janet Taylor Lisle	$2.75
❑ MT43109-9	**Boys Are Yucko** Anna Grossnickle Hines	$2.75
❑ MT43473-X	**The Broccoli Tapes** Jan Slepian	$2.95
❑ MT42709-1	**Christina's Ghost** Betty Ren Wright	$2.75
❑ MT43461-6	**The Dollhouse Murders** Betty Ren Wright	$2.75
❑ MT43444-6	**Ghosts Beneath Our Feet** Betty Ren Wright	$2.75
❑ MT44351-8	**Help! I'm a Prisoner in the Library** Eth Clifford	$2.75
❑ MT44567-7	**Leah's Song** Eth Clifford	$2.75
❑ MT43618-X	**Me and Katie (The Pest)** Ann M. Martin	$2.75
❑ MT41529-8	**My Sister, The Creep** Candice F. Ransom	$2.75
❑ MT42883-7	**Sixth Grade Can Really Kill You** Barthe DeClements	$2.75
❑ MT40409-1	**Sixth Grade Secrets** Louis Sachar	$2.75
❑ MT42882-9	**Sixth Grade Sleepover** Eve Bunting	$2.75
❑ MT41732-0	**Too Many Murphys** Colleen O'Shaughnessy McKenna	$2.75

Available wherever you buy books, or use this order form.

Scholastic Inc., P.O. Box 7502, 2931 East McCarty Street, Jefferson City, MO 65102

Please send me the books I have checked above. I am enclosing $_____ (please add $2.00 to cover shipping and handling). Send check or money order — no cash or C.O.D.s please.

Name _____

Address _____

City_____ State/Zip _____

Please allow four to six weeks for delivery. Offer good in the U.S.A. only. Sorry, mail orders are not available to residents of Canada. Prices subject to change.

APP591